D0200950

KING ARTHUR
and His Knights

All this time the hand and arm that held the sword remained quite still. (See page 53)

KING ARTHUR
and His Knights

BASED ON SIR THOMAS MALORY'S
MORTE d'ARTHUR

Compiled and arranged by
ELIZABETH LODOR MERCHANT

Illustrated

The John C. Winston Company
Philadelphia • *Toronto*

Illustrations and special features
© 1957, 1927, by THE JOHN C. WINSTON COMPANY

Made especially for
J. G. FERGUSON PUBLISHING COMPANY

Made in the United States of America
L. C. Card #57–12797

Contents

List of Illustrations

Introduction

THE court celebrates the king's birthday. Nobles in velvet and miniver, ladies in silks and jewels make the hall bright with color and gay with laughter, while swift servitors run back and forth with food and drink. Presently, at a sign from the king, one member of the group seats himself beside a golden harp and strikes a chord. In the silence that follows he lifts his voice in a chant of the great deeds of a hero king to which are likened the victories of the leader whose birthday is being celebrated. Applause interrupts the singer time and again as the story continues, for he sings the praise of Arthur, the hero most beloved of the people.

Where are we? In southern England perhaps, or in northern France, or, with somewhat less of luxury in the setting, in the Scotch Grampians, or the fastnesses of the Welsh mountains. And when? Any time through the run of the centuries from the twelfth to the sixteenth, or, indeed, earlier or later, if we shift somewhat our thought of singer and audience. The sounds may proceed from a venerable bard who sings prophetwise in a wild Welsh glen, from a minstrel whose welcome presence brightens the feudal hall of a Scotch fortress, from a fantastic jongleur who amuses his Norman host with alternate song and sleight-of-hand tricks, or, as we have suggested, from a courtly and renowned trouvère whom royalty greets with honor. We may well believe that echoes of the song come back to us from far and lonely places; fragments of it are on the lips of shepherd and swineherd or pass into everyday allusion in market place and in humble homes. In Celtic Britain of the sixth century, through the intervening years to our own time, we find it appearing and reappearing as a favored theme. Nor is it confined to Western Europe; in translations it is scattered far and wide; it is world literature, a quarry from which all modern peoples have hewn.

ix

This story, which has so deeply impressed itself upon the hearts and minds of men, centers in the shadowy but heroic figure of Arthur, king of the Britons in the fifth or sixth century. Its most important early form is the Latin of Geoffrey of Monmouth in his "Historia Britonum" (1130–1147). Told in courtly Norman French by Geoffrey Gaimar and again by Wace to please Queen Eleanor (1155); presently in English by Layamon in his "Brut" (1205); and then in a later English by Sir Thomas Malory (1469 or 1470), it flowed along through these three centuries. On its current it carried the elements of all the influences and ideals that were gradually determining the nature and standards of the English-speaking world.

Though minstrel and trouvère have long since vanished, and cold print has replaced chant and harp, there is no lack of visible tokens to recall the cherished legends. The sacred thorn still flowers at Glastonbury, the ruins of the castle called Arthur's still crown a Cornish cliff above the recesses of Merlin's Cave, and a Round Table at Winchester has a rival under the walls of Stirling Castle. These places revive for the visitor the interest and even the conviction of an earlier time and so stir his imagination that he hears the echo of ancient song or sees, as in "dim, rich" Camelot, the brave procession of Arthur's knights passing up to the great hall raised by Merlin's magic.

While students in the particular field of the Arthur tradition find a keen interest in sifting the mass of legends to discover the obscure facts behind them, most readers are satisfied to conclude that this kingly figure embodies what men would fain have seen brought to birth by the travail of their spirit had so fine a consummation been reached. We should like to know whether the Arthur story began in Cumbria and Strathclyde, travelling south, or began in Wales and drifted south and east and across the Channel, or began in Cornwall and moved east. Still more significant and arresting is the spectacle of the metamorphoses which it undergoes after it reaches the period of recorded literature. Stark trials of brute strength, courtly amours, religious ecstasy, a sense of social obligation, and visions of ideal justice emerge in the successive versions of the old tale. While you seize one aspect or another, it shifts under your grasp and takes on a different shape. In these variants there may be seen the ideals of the successive times that produced them.

Still another source of interest lies in the realization that these stories must have been a unifying influence in troubled medieval England. A Celtic king becomes the property of Saxon commons and Norman lords, and though each people may have claimed him as theirs, none the less he was a common standard, a rallying sign for a whole people. Stories about him were equally welcome in court and hovel. He gained a hold upon the affections and imagination of that varied, complex people exceeding in strength their devotion to the more real and tangible King Alfred. Alfred is solid fact, not the fluid material of tradition; what he actually did and was must remain. Perhaps for a similar reason the epic cycles of Alexander and Charlemagne lost their fascination when they were brought into the sobering light of day. At all events the Arthur story remains a triumphant, vitalizing force in the world of English literature.

Nor was its virtue spent in pre-Renaissance days. Milton dreamed of it as a subject for his life work; public life claimed him and the play was never written. The subject was a controlling life interest with Tennyson. As early as 1832 he published the "Lady of Shalott," his first poem drawn from this source. In 1888, after a labor of forty-six years, he concluded his majestic cycle of the "Idylls." Matthew Arnold, Charles Algernon Swinburne, and William Morris are other famous nineteenth century poets who, responding to the attraction of this romance, have contributed to the literature of the subject.

Among the multiplied recitals, two are most significant for the general reader, those of Malory in the fifteenth century and of Tennyson in the nineteenth. To Malory we owe the gift of the complete story in an English which differs little from our own. More accurately we should say that we owe it also to Caxton, whose scholarly discernment and devotion prompted the printing of Malory's book among the issues of his press at Westminster. From this source, chiefly, modern writers have drawn their materials.

We have already alluded to the changes made in the progress of the story from time to time. Some of these changes have added material as new interests have been swept into the current. The story of the Grail, for instance, seems to have appeared first in the version of Walter Map, or Mapes, a Welshman at the court of Henry II, who thus added a religious element to the tale. Changes in character interpretation and in underlying motives are very marked in modern versions. In Tennyson's "The Idylls of the King" a central theme welds the twelve poems into an epic whole, in which we may see how profoundly Tennyson's thought was influenced by contemporary scientific revelations. He shows the slow progress of man in his development as an individual and as a social unit, teaching the world to strive for clearer vision and steadier purpose, steadfast in spite of delay and error, firm in the belief that while

"The old order changeth, yielding place to new,"

it still is true that

"God fulfils himself in many ways
Lest one good custom should corrupt the world."

The Arthur story is classed as world literature; the term will bear emphasis. While it is true that all the world loves a story, it is also true that it loves particular stories above others. Cinderella, Beauty and the Beast, Puss-in-Boots, Jack the Giant Killer, dim and remote in origin, are known wherever childhood has its rightful heritage. What land has not its tales of fire-breathing dragons, enemies of mortals, to be conquered only by superhuman god-men? The battle cries of Homer's heroes still ring in modern ears after three thousand years of wars. Great chiefs, withdrawn from mortal knowledge, await the summons of their people alike in American Indian legends, in Teutonic sagas, and in Celtic prophecies. Certain fundamental ideas and interests awaken response in men of all times and places. They survive all changes and accompany all migrations, bearing testimony to the essential unity of human sympathies. They are significant, too, of the limited range of man's activities. A few good themes cover broadly all the stories that have ever been told. War, love, adventure, domestic life, community organization, the ways of the gods with men furnish the material for most of them, and these interests are permanent, implicit in life.

Like all other world literature, the Arthur story is woven of such threads, and, like them, draws these threads from various lands and races. It is not strange that the resultant fabric is rich in pattern and color. Many hands have spun the thread and guided the weaving, and through the loom the fabric is still passing, at once a heritage from the past and a promise of beauty yet to be.

Naturally, numerous versions for young people have been made. Elements of youth characterize all world literature. Action rather than reflection and a childlike directness enchain the attention of young imaginations. In "King Arthur and His Knights" these qualities are prominent and, combined with its happy phrasing, assure the popularity of the book.

—Elizabeth Lodor Merchant

The Two Dragons

". . . Merlin, the wise man that ever served King Uther thro' his magic art . . ."

MERLIN, the most famous magician of legend, even in his youth seemed to be unlike the ordinary boy, and a good many people said that he was half fairy and were rather afraid of him. He never did wicked or cruel things, but he would often rock his sides with laughter for what seemed to be no reason at all. Sometimes he would disappear for a week or two, and it was whispered of him that he would catch and ride the wild stags; and that, when he rode a great antlered beauty, all the pretty does and their young followed him, so that the forest glades seemed alive with flying herds of deer. The gossips said, too, that the fairy people were building a house for Merlin in the deep green places of the woods—a house with seventy windows and sixty doors—where, as soon as he was old enough, he would live quite alone. But

1

when Merlin was stared at on account of these things, he only laughed to himself, as usual, and, unconcerned, went about his business.

Then, one day, a party of horsemen came riding along toward the palace in which Merlin had been born. They asked all whom they met where they could find a certain handsome youth of whom many strange tales were told. The things they mentioned were exactly the stories that were told about Merlin; so, of course, everybody who answered the horsemen told them where Merlin could be found. And, curiously enough, as the riders drew rein before the gate of the city, there stood the slender boy with his laughing mouth and eyes so clear and wild and free.

One of the horsemen sprang down, seized Merlin, and flung him on his own saddle. Then he sprang up behind, set spurs to his steed, and galloped off in company with his friends. Merlin neither struggled nor cried out. He just laughed to himself as usual; for ever since he was a baby he had known that this would happen to him.

On went the party of horsemen at full speed until they came to a country far from Merlin's home. Between the mountain passes they rode and, presently, came out upon a low plain where hundreds of workmen were toiling and toiling and toiling to build a great tower. They had brought great piles of stones together, but these were lying about, broken or piled in muddled heaps. Men on horseback rode to and fro, calling out directions or rebuking the workmen for their carelessness. The poor workmen staggered about, placing the stones one on the top of the other. But however careful they were, or in whatever position they put them, the stones were no sooner set up than they, one and all, fell down again!

Watching the work from a grassy mound stood a tall man in armor, with a crown on his head and a cruel, yet frightened, face under the crown. Behind him waited a standard bearer in royal purple. And over his crowned head hung the flag that had floated over many a prince of a long, long line of kings.

The company of horsemen galloped up to the mound. Taking Merlin down from the horse, they led him, bound, up to the cruel-eyed monarch who stood there.

"Is this the boy?" asked the king. "You have found the child who was described to me?"

"Yes, sire," answered the rider who had first seized Merlin, "we have found him and brought him to you."

The king looked steadily and fiercely at Merlin, who smiled back pleasantly, not at all afraid.

"You laugh, child!" said the king, with a heavy frown. "You do not know your fate! Do you see those stones and that place where men have built the foundations of a great tower?"

Merlin nodded. He looked around at the heaps of unused stones, so many of which were broken and spoiled.

"In that tower," went on the king, "I mean to find a safe refuge from the terrible enemies who swarm on all sides of my country. These foes will, assuredly, ride one day over the mountains, and, unless I provide a safe retreat, will conquer my kingdom and kill me. Only a strong tower can be my haven. But, although I have tried for many months to build it, no sooner are the stones set up than they all fall down again!"

"I am not at all surprised to hear it," said Merlin, apparently little interested in what the king was saying.

"Wait!" growled the king, like angry thunder. "You will soon be less unconcerned. I was told by a magician that only the blood of a youth of whom it was said he was half a fairy could give firmness to the foundations of the tower. You, I understand, are that unhappy child! My tower I must have, though your blood be spilled in order to build it!"

Even this cruel king looked unhappy as well as alarmed as he spoke. But, in spite of all his sorrow and his fear, he was quite determined to kill Merlin so that he could go on building his tower.

Merlin laughed, bowed, and sat down on the grass of the mound, right under the royal purple flag that was held by the royal standard bearer.

"Indeed?" said he. "But even my blood, great King, will not help you to build a tower on the top of a lake of water!"

The king frowned with perplexity and stared at the boy who was said to be half a fairy.

"Lake of water! What do you mean?" he demanded. "There is no lake here—nothing but solid, red-brown earth."

"Set your workmen to dig around the foundations of your unfinished, tumbling-down tower and you will soon see for yourself," laughed Merlin, rocking himself to and fro, with his hands clasped about his knees.

The king—whose name was Vortigern—was so amazed that he actually did as the strange, mocking boy told him! He sent for the architect who was trying in vain to build the tower, and bade him order the workmen to dig around about the foundations with their spades. So the workmen stopped trying to set up the stones and began shoveling out the soil instead. And, behold! almost immediately they were digging in mud, and up bubbled the hidden water through the mud, and down fell the banks of the ditches, followed by all the stones that had not tumbled down before. And, as the stones and banks slipped down, more and more water rushed up, until at last the whole of the middle of the plain was one great lake from which the workmen were all running away in one direction and the architect and the horsemen in another. But King Vortigern and Merlin still sat together under the royal standard on the grassy summit of the mound, gazing earnestly at the enormous lake.

Then the king turned to Merlin, more afraid, now, of this strange, laughing boy than of all the people whom he expected to come riding over the hills to kill him and seize his kingdom.

"What does it all mean?" he asked, trembling. "What does it all mean?"

Merlin shook his head. Suddenly tears sprang to his eyes and rolled down his cheeks. He was sorry for the cruel king, though Vortigern had never been sorry for him.

"There is a great stone below the lake," he said, in a whisper. "Two dragons sleep there— one red and one white. One day they will come out from under the stone and meet on the waters of the lake in a fearful battle. In the white dragon is the soul of your strongest enemy— in the red dragon you may see the reflection of yourself."

Then Merlin stepped down from the mound and went slowly away, and nobody tried to hold him. But Vortigern sat on the grass and stared for a week on end at the still green waters of the magical lake.

And at last, while he stared, he saw the waters shudder and break into great waves. The waves sprang higher and higher and broke into foamy strands, looking like the white and shaggy manes of horses tossed by the wind. Then up through the hills and valleys of the storm-lashed water came the white dragon and the red dragon. The white dragon was as pale as snow, and the red dragon was as scarlet as blood. Their

With a great cry, the red dragon fell dead upon the beach.

wings, high above the angry waves, looked like crimson and silver clouds flying low across the sky. And from end to end of the fairy lake they fought each other, until, with a great cry, the red dragon fell dead upon the beach among the green rushes and the broken stems of the water flowers.

Vortigern rose and fled. But he thought he heard the voice of the fairy boy echoing all round about him as he went:

"In the white dragon is the soul of your strongest enemy—in the red dragon you may see the reflection of yourself!"

The king arrived at his palace quaking with fear, but lo! his courtiers came running to tell him that the lake had sunk back deep into the earth, and that now the workmen were building his tower as fast as ever they could. So Vortigern began his old cruel, wicked ways once more. Then, as soon as the tower was finished, he shut himself up in it for safety. But at night, very often, he woke up panting with terror, for, in his dreams, he had seen again the mighty battle between the white dragon and the red dragon.

And, as he had feared, one day his strongest enemy came over the hills with a great army, for Vortigern's people, racked with their king's wickedness and cruelty, had sent out a pitiful cry for help. The king who rode over the hills was great and good, and he rescued the unhappy people, and then went to the big tower and bade Vortigern come out. There was no answer from inside, and so the soldiers set fire to the tower, and it blazed fiercely for days and days, until at last the walls were all burned away. Nothing was left but a heap of ruins lying on the very spot where the red dragon had fallen dead after the great fight with the white dragon on the lake.

Vortigern had been shut up in the tower all this time, so that it happened that he was killed by the great king just as the red dragon had been killed by the white. But nobody could be sorry, for he had been cruel to everyone and would have willingly slain Merlin to save his own wicked life. So the good king reigned over the kingdom in his place, and was called Uther Pendragon. The reasons for this name and some of the things that Uther did you will read about in another story.

The
Holy Grail

"The cup, the cup itself, from which our Lord
Drank at the last sad supper with His own.
This . . . the good saint
Arimathæan Joseph, journeying brought
To Glastonbury, where the winter thorn
Blossoms at Christmas, mindful of our Lord."

LONG before Merlin was born there lived, in an Eastern country, a good and holy man called Joseph, who had, for many years, been the guardian of a wonderful cup. Nobody quite knew whence his cup had first come, nor who had made it, nor what gave it the lovely radiance which always surrounded it and made it look more beautiful than any fairy goblet set with emeralds and pearls. But all Joseph's friends knew that the cup was a great treasure, and that only a good and faithful man could have been chosen as its guardian. So they honored and respected Joseph, and talked reverently of the precious chalice of which he had the care.

This cup was called the Grail Cup, and sometimes Joseph would summon his children and his grandchildren (for he was quite an old man) and the best loved of his friends to take their seats at a Silver Table which he himself had made, in the middle of which he would set the Grail Cup. Then, while everyone looked at the shining mist in which the cup was half hidden, Joseph would tell another good man, called Alan, whom he loved very dearly, to go to a certain stream and catch a silver fish that he would see swimming about in the clear water. Alan would go willingly; and, however often he went, he always saw the silver fish gleaming and flashing among the singing bubbles of the stream. He would catch the fish and bring it to the bright table to show to Joseph, who would then tell him to take it and broil it on a fire of clear embers. When this was done, Alan served the fish to the people who sat about the Silver Table. No matter how many there were to feed, there was always enough, and, when the feast was over, all who had shared in it felt revived, content, and joyful, strong to do what was right and to resist what was wrong. They would go away glad and grateful, wondering how it was that Alan could always catch so magical and marvelous a fish. They never really understood the secret, which belonged to Alan and Joseph alone; but they gave Alan the name of the Rich Fisher, and as the Rich Fisher he has been known for many hundreds of years.

So it happened that month after month the Silver Table was spread, the Grail Cup was displayed, and the mysterious fish was served by the Rich Fisher. But wicked men ruled the country in which Joseph lived, and they had already once thrown him into prison because he would not give up his cup. They were again plotting against him, when, one day as he worked in his garden, he was visited by a beautiful spirit who told him that he must take the Grail to a distant country called West-over-the-Sea. Joseph asked how this could be done. "For," said he, "I am only a gardener and a worker in the cornfields, and I have no ship in which to voyage nor sailor friends to manage its oars and sails." The bright spirit, however, bade him have faith and not be afraid. He was trustfully to set off with his children and his friends, and they were to carry the Silver Table and the Shining Cup with them. Then the vision faded away among the vines and dark cedar trees, and Joseph went into his house and, sending for the Rich Fisher, told him and everybody else to make ready for the journey.

Well, they set off as soon as they could, Joseph, the Rich Fisher, their children, and their friends. With tender care they carried the Silver Table, and Joseph bore the Shining Cup in a casket set with hundreds of precious stones. After traveling for many days, they reached the seashore. There lay the deep blue ocean ahead of them, rosy-purple in the far distance, and

overhung with the clouds of sunset that, delicate
and golden, looked like enchanted islands. One
of these, everybody felt quite sure, must be the
home chosen for the Grail Cup.

But between them and the enchanted islands
of the sunset the sea rolled its long, murmuring,
restless waves. Not a sail was to be seen; not a
single little boat rocked in the green furrows
near the shore. Joseph stood at the edge of the
water, perplexed and wondering, and the sunset
light fell on his white underrobe and scarlet
mantle. As he stood, with everybody silently
watching him, a voice suddenly floated across the
shore.

"Take off your white underrobe, Joseph,"
said the voice, "and spread it upon the sea."

Joseph bowed his head, and, while his people
gazed in wonder, he took off his white underrobe, and, stepping into the ripples, spread the
soft finely-sewn linen out upon the water. It
floated like a beautiful raft, spreading wider and
wider on the waves, and Joseph heard the voice
a second time, falling as musically as the song
of a bird through the quiet evening air.

"Step forward and take your stand upon it,
and let all your people follow you."

Joseph moved forward and, lifting high the
casket which held the Grail Cup, stepped upon
this strange white boat. The linen garment was
firm to his feet, and rocked up and down like a
strong ship at anchor. He stood there, fearless
and upright, and called to all his people to join

him. In twos and threes they came, amazed but
trustful, bringing with them the Silver Table,
while Joseph still held up the casket in which
the Shining Cup was safely hidden. Room was
found for everyone upon the floating white robe,
and the Silver Table was set in the very middle.
Then, as soon as his people had gathered around
Joseph, some strange power stirred the quiet ripples of the sea, the linen robe began to move
from the shore, and, in a very few minutes, the
Keeper of the Grail Cup, Alan the Rich Fisher,
and all their children and grandchildren found
themselves traveling swiftly and smoothly
across the ocean in the direction of West-over-
the-Sea.

The sun sank, the moon rose, and still the
white linen robe, with all these people clustered
together upon it, sailed, faster than any ship,
over the starlit water. Then, by and by, the moon
set, too, and the sun climbed again into the sky
behind the travelers. As it rose, it threw its
golden beams upon the fresh and fragrant, still
drowsy, world, and Joseph cried out joyfully that
he could see the sandy beaches, the high cliffs,
and the distant mountains of West-over-the-Sea.

And there, like a costly gem in a setting of
polished silver, lay the land, sparkling and beautiful. But, as the travelers drew nearer, they
saw that while they had left warmth and flowers
and fruiting trees behind them, they had come
to a country where winter reigned. This land
was cold and snow covered. The rocks glittered

with the frosts of the night; the streams were hushed under the silence of the ice. The outspread robe floated into a little bay, and the chill winds of the north blew upon the voyagers' faces, as, one by one, they stepped down into the icy ripples and hurried breathlessly to the shore.

Joseph came last of all, and, as he left his strange ship, the voice came again, down from the mountains, telling him to lift his robe and put it once more upon his shoulders. He did so, and, behold! it was quite warm and dry. Then he and the Rich Fisher led all the people up a narrow pathway which climbed the cliff side. And still Joseph bore the Grail, while some of the others willingly carried the Silver Table between them.

They reached the top of the cliff, and then they traveled onward, over rugged mountains and through peaceful valleys, until they reached a place called Glastonbury. And Joseph knew that here he was meant to build a little church of wood. He leaned on his staff for a long time, looking about him with joy in his eyes. It seemed to him a wonderful thing that he was to build a church in the island of Britain, which was the real name of West-over-the-Sea.

Then, as he leaned on his staff, he felt it move and tremble strangely under his hand. He glanced down, and lo! he saw little twigs and stems laden with green leaves and pale whitethorn flowers sprouting out on all sides of the staff. Taking his hand from it, startled, he per-

ceived that it had rooted in the frost-bound
earth! Wonderingly he touched the tiny flowers,
and, even as he touched them, snow began to
fall and mingle its feathery flakes with the
pearly petals. Then the staff shot upward, and
great boughs, fully clothed with blossoms,
branched about Joseph's figure and high above
his head. In a few minutes he was standing,
amazed, under a spreading thorn tree, laden
with sweet-smelling snow-white bloom!

Then Joseph called the Rich Fisher to him.
He called, too, to all his followers—who stood as
amazed as himself—and told them to set down
the Silver Table under the flowering tree. They
did so, and the Rich Fisher, in obedience to Joseph, went to a little half-frozen stream close at
hand. There, swimming about close to the edge
of the ice, he saw the beautiful gleaming fish.
Quickly he caught it, and, making a fire of sticks,
roasted it upon the clear embers. Then, coming
back to the Silver Table, he saw that Joseph had
set the Shining Cup in the center of it, and that
everyone was prepared to share in the magical
feast. So there, under the blossoming thorn
tree, the children and followers of Joseph and
the Rich Fisher ate their first banquet at West-
over-the-Sea, while the snow fell thickly all about
them and covered the fields and plain of Glastonbury with a mantle of purity.

Now, while they were feasting, an old man
dressed in a long robe, who was called a Druid,
passed by and paused, utterly amazed at what

he saw. Well might he be surprised to see these
Eastern people, in their blue and purple and
scarlet robes, seated around a Silver Table under
a tree covered with flowers. He, with a strange
feeling of awe, gazed at them and at a beautiful
cup which was set in the middle of the table and
which shone as delicately as a little moonlit cloud.
Even while he watched, the banquet came to an
end. The strangers stood up; the one who seemed
to be chief took the cup into his hands; others
lifted the Silver Table; and, unaware that they
were seen by the old Druid, they all swept away
in a radiant procession toward the inland forests,
leaving the blossoming tree standing, mysterious and beautiful, under the falling snow.

The Druid stepped up to the tree, touched it,
and smelled the flowers. Then he went back to
the grove of oaks in which he lived, and wrote
down all that he had seen in a parchment book
fastened with gold clasps. This book he locked
up, and it was kept hidden for many years; but
Merlin heard of it, and, one day, long, long afterward, he came to Glastonbury, found it, and read
it. What he did, after he had read the book, you
will be told in another story. But meanwhile,
Joseph and the Rich Fisher and their friends
sought the king of the country, and he gave
them for their own the piece of land where
the thorn tree was blossoming. So they built
a little wooden church there, and the country
people worshiped in it for many years.

Merlin with his snow-white beard came slowly up the room.

The Dragon
in the Sky

"Sir," said Merlin, "I know all your heart, every deal; so ye will be sworn unto me as ye are a true king anointed, to fulfil my desire, ye shall have your desire . . . ye shall deliver the child to me to nourish as I will have it; for it shall be to your worship, and the child's avail as mickle as the child is worth."

ONE dark night while a storm was raging, Merlin stood at one of his seventy windows and looked and looked and looked up at the wild sky. He was expecting to see something there, something very unusual and wonderful, which one of his fairy books had told him to expect. For a long time, however, nothing happened. The watching magician saw only the clouds racing like inky shadows over the clear, high spaces that were sprinkled with stars. Then, suddenly, he caught sight of a little pearly glimmer in the north. This little pearly glimmer grew brighter and brighter; it turned from silver to gold, and from gold to a deep shining red, like the red of rubies. Merlin gazed still more

eagerly, and presently, in the heart of the red
glow, he saw a great star brighten, as you might
see a crimson spark suddenly break into a shining flame. From the great star one ray shot
out suddenly, brilliant as a diamond and slender
as a knight's spear. At the end of the ray appeared a globe of fire, which, as Merlin still
watched, uncoiled itself slowly and took the
shape of a beautiful but terrifying dragon. This
fiery dragon opened its mouth and sent out two
more rays, one to the east, the other to the west.
The eastern ray seemed to have no end, but
spread out into a great glow so that you might
almost have thought the sun was just about to
rise. The ray to the west led into the night shadows and then broke up into seven smaller rays
which spread themselves in a golden fan above
the shadowy peaks of the distant hills.

When Merlin had seen all this happen, he
laughed gladly, and, flying down the long staircase of his fairy home, as lightly as a bird or a
butterfly, he set off on invisible wings through
the night. Always the fiery dragon shone in the
sky overhead, and Merlin knew that its bright
form was hanging just over the castle of Uther,
the king. As the wizard drew near to the castle
he dropped to his feet on the grass and took on
the form of an old man wrapped in a cloak. With
his white beard blowing about him in the wind,
and the hood of the cloak drawn down over his
eyes and forehead, Merlin walked up to the
castle gates and knocked loudly with his staff.

Now all this time the great, flaming dragon was lying stretched out in the sky, bathing the towers and turrets of the castle in a crimson light, fiery and frightful. The guards and servants, the porters, the cooks, and the pages had seen it, and were very, very much frightened. Nobody dared to answer the door at first, so Merlin knocked again much more loudly. Then, when a terrified porter appeared, the magician, in a voice of authority, demanded to be taken to the presence of the king.

There was something in Merlin's voice that the porter dared not disobey. He hurriedly opened the great gate and let the old man in. Then he led Merlin through the courtyard—all aglow with the dragon's light—down the great stone corridor, across the hall hung with gorgeous tapestry, where trembling pages waited, dressed in satins and silks. There the porter paused and pointed, and Merlin went on alone right into the royal apartment of the king.

King Uther sat on his throne, pale and grave and quite alone. Through a great window, curtainless and arched, came the fiery glow from the dragon in the sky. It stained the fresh green rushes on the floor with crimson, and shone all about the solitary figure of the king. Uther looked up at the sound of footsteps and saw an old man coming slowly up the room, wrapped in a long cloak, with a snow-white beard that streamed, in long thick strands, far below his waist.

"Who are you? Why do you come here un-
bidden and unannounced?" demanded the king
sternly. But, before he finished speaking, the
old man threw back his cloak, and Uther saw
who he was.

"Merlin—my friend Merlin!" he cried in an
altered voice. "I am indeed glad you have come!
What means this blazing and terrifying dragon
in the sky? Is it a sign of some cruel disaster,
some great trouble, that is about to fall upon
my house?"

Then Merlin answered. His voice sounded
so joyous and triumphant that King Uther knew
the news was good even before the magician
spoke.

"The dragon is the most wonderful sign that
has ever shone in the sky above the castle of a
king," cried Merlin. "I have been watching for
it night after night, hoping and longing to see
it come! It means that to you, and to the beautiful lady you love, a little prince will be born.
This little prince will be the greatest king the
world ever saw. He will reign over many sub-
jects and will conquer all his enemies. He is the
ray that goes from the mouth of the dragon to
the east, and he will be as bright and beautiful
as the rising sun. The ray that goes to the west,
and breaks up into seven rays, is your daughter.
She will be not only a princess but a fairy, and
have seven fairy children, who will teach the
men-children of the West the songs that fairies
sing. See how the seven rays end in a shining

mist! That is the meaning of the fiery dragon,
King Uther—the meaning that I have hurried
into your presence to explain!"

Uther listened breathlessly, while the light
from the dragon shone crimson upon the faces
and hands and robes of the old wizard and the
young king. Then Uther leaned forward and
pressed his fingers on Merlin's arm.

"My 'beautiful lady'?" he said eagerly. "Do
you mean Ygierne?"

He could hardly wait for Merlin's reply, because he had loved Ygierne for many months,
but she was shut up in a castle, quite out of his
reach.

"Yes, I mean Ygierne," answered Merlin. "I
promise that you shall have her for your bride.
I promise, too, that you and she shall have this
bright and beautiful prince and this fairylike
princess for your children. But, if you are to
marry Ygierne through my help, you must make
me a promise in return."

"What is that?" asked Uther. "Tell me!
There is no promise that I would not make for
the sake of beautiful Ygierne!"

"You must promise that, as soon as your
little son is born, you will give him into my care.
He has a great work to do in the world, and can
learn to do it only if I have the care of him.
Give me your promise, Uther, and I will set about
the performance of mine!"

Then King Uther, for a moment, felt uncer-
tain and sad. Where would be the gladness in a

little princely son if the child was to be taken
away from him as soon as he was born? But he
loved Ygierne so passionately that, after hesitating for only one second, he consented.

"Very well, Merlin!" he cried. "Very well!
You shall have my little son to bring up as your
own child, if you will only make it possible for
me to marry my beautiful lady Ygierne!"

The red light shining through the window,
that fell from the fiery dragon in the sky, grew
stronger and fiercer as Uther spoke. When he
had given the promise, the light blazed crimson
and awful about the throne on which he sat, and
glistened upon all the diamonds and sapphires
in his scepter and crown. A peal of thunder
rolled above the palace; a flash of lightning
darted about the gray stone towers. The blazing
dragon seemed to close its jaws. As it closed
them the rays drew slowly back into its great
mouth—the one ray from the east, and the seven
rays from the west. It stretched out its long
fiery claws, and two great golden wings rose,
waving, over its great golden head. Then, for
an instant, it spread out these wings and hung
poised above the castle, so that all the pages and
cooks and scullions and porters hid themselves
in the darkest corners and cupboards and cellars
they could find. But, instead of swooping down
upon the castle, as they expected, the blazing
dragon struck its wings together once—twice—
thrice. Once, twice, thrice the thunder pealed
out again; and, before its echoes had died away,

the fiery creature had shot, swift as an arrow, far through the night sky, leaving behind it a long tail of starry light, like the tail of a comet.

Even King Uther had crouched for a moment and covered his face. When he took his jeweled satin cloak from his eyes the royal throne room was empty, dark, and still. Merlin had vanished with the dragon, and had gone back to the fairy house of seventy windows and sixty doors. The king was left alone, with the promise of a beautiful bride and a wonderful little son.

The king stepped down from his throne and went to the window. He looked up to the sky, and saw it dark and clear, silvered over with little quiet stars. Then he summoned a herald (who came, still trembling) and told him to take his trumpet and go through the castle, crying aloud these words:

"King Uther has been told the meaning of the blazing dragon in the sky. It is a sign of great gladness and victory and well-being for himself and for his kingdom. From now the king will be known as King Uther Pendragon, and he lays commands on his royal sculptors that two golden dragons immediately be made. One of these dragons will be set up in the capital of his kingdom. The other will be carried by his royal standard-bearer into every battle. These are the orders of Uther Pendragon, king of the lordly and ancient country of Britain!"

The Sword
of the King

"And when matins and the first mass was done, there was seen in the churchyard, against the high altar, a great stone four square, like unto a marble stone, and in midst thereof was like an anvil of steel a foot on high, and therein stuck a fair sword naked by the point, and letters there were written in gold about the sword that said thus: Whoso pulleth out this sword of this stone and anvil, is rightwise king born of all England."

IN DUE time Merlin kept his promise to King Uther. It so happened that Gorlois, Duke of Cornwall, who had kept Ygierne shut up in his castle, was overthrown and slain in battle, and Uther became owner of the castle.

All that Merlin had promised now came true, and Uther hastened to visit his beloved, winsome Ygierne, and to tell her that he loved her and would always protect her. So she married him, and became his queen.

After the marriage, King Uther Pendragon and his sweet and lovely lady Ygierne lived very

26

happily in Tintagel Castle by the Cornish Sea.
You may see the ruins of it now, but you can
never imagine perhaps how fine and strong it
was in those days, hundreds of years ago. Massive gray towers rose above great gray roofs,
and archers practiced shooting from the strong,
high walls. Sometimes the big gates and doors
were closed—sometimes they opened wide to let
out large companies of soldiers, dressed in
bright armor and riding on handsome, spirited
horses with gay bridles and reins. In the evenings sounds of music and laughter came from
inside. Minstrels with harps played and sang to
the king and queen; and funny dwarfs, in caps
and bells, made jokes, or danced absurd little
dances among the rushes on the floor. Oh, it
was a wonderful place, was Tintagel, and you
will never see anything like it nowadays! Folks
were brave and cheerful then, and, though they
no doubt had terrific battles with their neigh-
bors, they were so gay and courageous between
times that their lives passed as happily as possible, what with work and play, banquets and
tournaments. The knights loved and fought for
the fair ladies. The fair ladies loved and looked
after the knights. And, bravest, most loving,
and fairest of all, were King Uther Pendragon
and Ygierne, the queen.

As the days passed they were very happy together at Tintagel, and by and by their little
son was born. Poor Ygierne was now told that
Uther had promised to give the baby instantly

into Merlin's charge. She was very sad about this, but she would not ask the king to break his word. Besides, she and Uther had often talked of the great future which Merlin had foretold for their child. So the king and queen kissed the baby prince, and the queen herself wrapped him up in a beautiful cloak of cloth of gold and gave him into the charge of two ladies and two knights. Then Uther told the two ladies and the two knights to carry the tiny prince to a certain little half-hidden door in the castle wall, to open this door softly and silently, and to give the child into the arms of somebody who would be waiting just outside to receive it.

Singing little soft lullabies, the two ladies stepped carefully down the corridor, followed by the two knights. They reached the winding stairs and went down, down, down to the little half-hidden door. On a golden cushion one lady carried the sleeping baby in its golden cloak. The other carried a tall candle; and the two knights, walking behind, carried two more candles, taller still, which cast strange, wavering shadows on the gray walls.

They opened the door, and the light of the candles shone out into the dark, still night. From among the shadows came a dim, tall figure, not unlike a shadow itself. This figure held out its hands for the baby, and the ladies and the knights without a word gave the tiny boy into the mysterious stranger's arms. And thus was Arthur

The ladies and the knights gave the tiny boy into the stranger's arms.

> "All as soon as born
> Delivered at a secret postern gate
> To Merlin, to be holden far apart
> Until his hour should come."

Then they went back through the door with their candles and the empty golden cushion; and, as they climbed up, up, up the winding staircase, they heard slowly dying in the distance the sound of the footsteps of a trotting horse.

On the horse rode Merlin with the baby. Over hill and dale he went until he reached a quiet, small castle in a valley. Here lived a good and sober knight called Sir Hector, who knew well why Merlin had come. Long ago, the magician and King Uther had sent for Sir Hector, and asked him if he would receive a little child into his house—a little child who was to become very great and famous, but who must be brought up simply as a noble knight's son. Sir Hector had consented, and had been given lands and riches in return. So, when Merlin rode up in the dark night, Sir Hector and his wife met the magician gladly and took the baby straight to their own nursery. Then Merlin had the little prince christened "Arthur"; and Sir Hector brought him up in his own good, peaceful, and happy home.

But Merlin was always at hand, watching over the boy. His father, King Uther, was content to leave little Arthur in the great wizard's charge. However, when he was dying, he sent for Merlin and asked for news of the child.

How happy he was when he heard that Prince
Arthur was growing up into a beautiful little
boy, already asking to ride his horse, hunt his
hounds, and shoot his arrows with the others.
How much better it was that he should, later,
be brought up just as a good knight instead of
as a king's favored son! Uther listened happily, certain now that his sacrifice of his baby
had not been made in vain. Then he gave back
to Merlin the Round Table which, as you shall
hear, had been placed in his care, and told him
how it might be kept safe and sound until Arthur
came into his kingdom. Accordingly, Merlin
had it carried far away to Cameliard, where it
was placed in the care of an old friend of Uther's,
another great king whose name was Leodogran,
who, in his turn, gave it into the charge of two
hundred and fifty knights, all of them brave,
noble, and good. What happened to it afterward
you will hear in another story.

So Uther died, but nobody knew that the
little lad in Sir Hector's house was the dead
king's son and heir. The barons of the country
began to quarrel, tooth and nail, among themselves. Each of them wanted the power to rule
over the rest. Never was there such an uncom-
fortable commotion! Wherever you went you
would meet soldiers on horseback, shaking their
spears and shouting out fine speeches about their
own baron and angry speeches about the barons
of other people. The woods and the meadows
rang with the sound of steel and the thunder of

horses' feet, so that at last Merlin went to the Archbishop, who mourned over these things very sorrowfully in his lonely palace of peace, and told him to call all the warring barons to London for Christmas, that they might go to service in the church and forget their quarrels, if it were only for the short and gentle hours of Christmas Day.

The barons dared not disobey the Archbishop, so to London and to church they duly went. After the service, out streamed the congregation into the churchyard. And there they saw something that had assuredly not been visible when they went in.

At the extreme east end of the churchyard, lit by the pale Christmas sun, stood a stone as white as marble, but a thousand times more beautiful. In the center of it was a square of steel like an anvil, and from the steel rose the glittering handle of a strong, sharp sword. In letters of gold about the sword were written strange and thrilling words—words which said that whoever could draw the sword out of the stone was King of Britain, Uther Pendragon's only rightful heir.

The barons crowded around the stone, wide-eyed and amazed. Each called out that he, if given a chance, was certainly the one and only chieftain who could draw the sword from the stone. Smiling oddly, Merlin, who stood near, bade them all try. Jostling one another in their hurry, they sprang, one by one, to the side of the stone, seized the handle of the sword, and pulled and tugged with all their might. But their efforts met with no success. The sword did not even tremble in its square of steel, while the gleaming golden letters written around it seemed to mock the barons with their quiet, sure message.

At last the barons, tired and angry, went away from the churchyard and began to amuse themselves by holding a tournament in some meadows not very far away. After all, it was Christmas time—the season for junketings, jousts, and knightly games. And, riding to the tournament as a matter of course came Sir Hector, his son Sir Kay, and the fair and noble boy Arthur, whom Sir Hector loved as much as his own child.

As they passed the churchyard they saw the sword, shining always in the stone that was like beautiful white marble, and they spoke to each other of the strangeness of the sight. Then they trotted forward, each on a handsome horse. But just as they were about to ride into the meadow, so bright with banners and gay voices, Sir Kay exclaimed, in utter dismay, that he could take no share in the delights of the tournament, for he had left his own sword at home!

"Turn your horse quickly, my son," said Sir Hector to young Arthur. "Gallop home and bring your brother's sword. You are too young for the knightly games, but he must on no account be left out of them."

Arthur did not wait to be told a second time. Home he went, at full speed, to fetch his elder "brother's" sword. But, when he reached the house, everything was lonely and locked up. Sir Hector's lady had gone to the tournament herself and had taken all the servants with her.

For a minute or two Arthur hesitated. Then he was struck by the very happiest thought. "I will go to the churchyard," said he, "and take the sword that is sticking out of the big white stone! It will do just as well for my brother as his own!"

So he mounted his horse again, and off to the churchyard he rode. Dismounting, he hastened to the great stone. There, not even pausing to read the words which were written in the golden letters, he took the sword by the handle and pulled. Lo and behold! the sword came as easily and lightly from the steel in the middle of the marble as a rose is plucked from the delicate green shelter of its bush.

Sword in hand, Arthur once more sprang into the saddle, and galloped away to the tournament. Over the meadow grass he trotted, and straight into the hands of Sir Kay he gave the sword. Then, like the light-hearted modest boy he was, he fell back among the other younglings, watching to see his elder brother's triumph, with an eager and delighted expectancy.

But Sir Kay was staring with all his eyes at the sword. He turned it this way and that, then rode off to where his father, also, watched from a distance.

"Sir," he said to Sir Hector, "this sword which young Arthur has brought me is the very sword that no baron could draw from the stone in the east of the churchyard! You have heard what was written around it in letters of gold?"

"I have heard," said Sir Hector, grave and startled. For he, too, had been told the story of the sword set so firmly in the beautiful white stone. He too, recognized the fair blade as it glittered in his son's hand.

"If this is so, sir," cried Sir Kay, with a glowing face, "then I—*I*—must be King of Britain, Uther Pendragon's heir!"

But Sir Hector, deep in thought, had turned his horse's head.

"Call your brother Arthur," he said, "and both of you follow me."

In silence he rode to the churchyard, and in silence Kay and Arthur followed him. When they had all dismounted near the stone, Sir Hector looked at Arthur, who stood quietly by.

"Put the sword back again!" said he. And Arthur did so.

Sir Hector turned then to Sir Kay.

"Draw it out," he commanded. But Sir Kay, when he put his hand to the sword, could no more do this than any of the barons who had tried so hard.

Then Sir Hector himself tried, and also failed. Tenderly he laid his hand on Arthur's shoulder.

"It is your turn, now. Show me—show your brother—the truth!"

So Arthur, still quite simply and naturally, reached out his young, quick fingers and, taking the sword for the second time from the shining white stone, would have given it into Sir Hector's hand. But Sir Hector instead of taking the sword, bent on one knee and did Arthur homage, as all good knights do homage to their liege lord and king.

"My son," said he, "and that I cannot help calling you, though you are not my son—the writing in the golden letters was set down on the marble slab for you! Hail, Arthur, son of Uther Pendragon, and King of Britain! Receive, before all others, the loyalty of those who love you best! Sir Hector, whom you have called 'father' and his son, your brother, Sir Kay."

The Table Round

"It was the time when first the question rose
About the founding of a Table Round,
That was to be, for love of God and men
And noble deeds, the flower of all the world;
And each incited each to noble deeds."

As LONG as Uther, Arthur's father, lived, Merlin, the great wizard, was always his best friend. The stories told about the magician's fairy house in the woods were quite true; and Merlin spent most of his time in his wonderful home among the pine trees, looking from one or another of the seventy windows, or passing in and out of one or another of the sixty doors. What a strange, shadowy place it was, to be sure, with wild deer feeding in the glades that surrounded it and wild geese clanging as they flew in flocks across the sky at night. Human beings never ventured very far into this mysterious wood, but they whispered many strange tales about it to one another as they sat over their big

log fires in the evenings. They named it the
Enchanted Forest, or, sometimes, the Valley of
No Return. Hunters who followed the hares
over the meadows, or chased the wild boars
through the tangled thickets on the edge of the
woodland, always stopped short and turned their
horses and their hounds about when they looked
into the dark shadows of these haunted trees.
Sometimes they caught glimpses of gray, dim
walls and towers, and heard sounds like fairies
singing or unseen horses trampling or invisible
hounds baying through the wood. Then the real
horses and hounds would begin to tremble as
the hunters hurried them away. But nobody
could ever quite describe what he had seen and
heard, though all were agreed that, if any rash
person ventured up to the dim, gray walls of
Merlin's home, something dreadful would happen to him.

In this hidden house, then, Merlin learned
many and varied things from the fairies, because he could see and hear and speak to the
invisible people of the air. He learned so many
of their secrets that at last he became a real
fairy king among them. Not only would the
wild stags carry him wherever he wanted to go,
but all the good fairy folk would come up out of
the streams and down from the stars whenever
he called them.

One day Merlin was standing under a great
oak tree just after the sun had set and the quiet
shadows had commenced to steal through his

beautiful wood. The little birds had stopped
singing, and the bats were beginning to flit
about. Merlin felt that something very wonderful was going to happen—something beautiful and strange, by which even the fairy folk
of the Enchanted Forest would be greatly
amazed. The evening grew darker, and, presently, the oak boughs above his head began to
rustle and whisper as if a little wind were waft-
ing them up and down. At the same time he
heard gentle tappings inside the tree trunk, and
a murmur of many voices speaking together in
what, to him, seemed to be an unknown foreign
tongue.

Then, in the middle of the shadows, the
branches and trunk of the oak began to give
out a silver light, like the shining of a full moon.
Slowly and silently the silvery light grew round
about the tree. The boughs seemed to fade
away, and a wonderful picture, as though it were
painted on the silvery mist, appeared—the picture of an old man with a long white beard,
standing before a Silver Table on which was set
a mysterious and beautiful Shining Cup. Round
about the table were seated many people who
wore gay Eastern robes and looked very calm
and happy. And, by the side of the old man
with the white beard, stood a younger man with
a silver fish in his hands. He placed the fish on
the table, and all stood up. Merlin thought he
heard them singing as they did so, but the music
was very faint and seemed to come from very

far away. Then the whole bright vision faded;
the Silver Table, and the Shining Cup, and the
gaily dressed people disappeared, and Merlin
found himself alone in the forest again with the
oak leaves whispering and rustling above his
head.

But, while he stood wondering, behold! a
little book suddenly fell down from the branches
close to his feet. As it fell he heard a gentle
voice speaking softly among the leaves of the
tree:

"In the little book is written the story of the
Silver Table and the Shining Cup that you have
been allowed to see in a vision! I, who speak
to you, am the old Druid who saw them brought
to the land of West-over-the-Sea. I have been
commanded to show you the vision, and to give
you the little book. Also I have been commanded
to tell you that from the wood of the oak tree in
whose boughs you have seen the vision you are
to carve another Round Table, like the Silver
Table on which the Shining Cup stood. When
you have carved this second Round Table, you
are to take it to King Uther and bid him keep
it carefully in his palace until his death. For it
will have a marvelous meaning and purpose for
many years to come."

The voice died away, and even Merlin, magician though he was, could not see the spirit of
the old Druid which had visited him in the Enchanted Forest and brought the little old mysterious book. But he picked up the book and

took it home to his fairy house. There he lit his
lamp, and, sitting down among his magic vol-
umes and crystals and strange caskets and
boxes, he read the book from end to end. And
in it was the whole story of Joseph and his followers, and the church made of wood at Glastonbury, and the beautiful Christmas flowering
thorn. Not only was the whole tale written
down in the book, but there were also careful
directions about the making of the second
Round Table which was to be carved from the
oak in whose branches Merlin had seen the vision, and, when finished, given into the care of
Uther, the king.

Merlin locked the book up carefully in one
of his caskets, for he knew what a very, very
precious possession it was. Many years afterward, the little book fell into the hands of another good old man who was very like the long-
dead Glastonbury Druid himself. It came to
him just as it came to Merlin, falling from the
boughs of a tree that was lit up with mysterious
light while a voice spoke softly among the rustling leaves. And—so people would have told
you in those days—it was through the writing in
the little old book that they knew all about the
Silver Table, and the Rich Fisher, and the hidden
secrets of the Holy Grail.

Meanwhile, however, Merlin kept the little
book locked up, and set to work to make a huge
Round Table from the oak tree in the wood.
Nobody knows exactly how he made it, but the

fairy folk helped him, and he found words written in the little book that were obeyed by invisible hands using invisible axes and saws and hammers and nails. When he had finished he was an even greater magician than he had been when he had begun—so great that, by using certain spells, he was able to lift the Round Table out of his house in the Enchanted Forest, and to set it down in the very middle of the great hall of the royal castle that belonged to Uther, the king.

Uther was greatly amazed when he saw this beautiful Round Table, brought to his castle nobody knew how. As he gazed at it, however, he became aware that Merlin was standing by him, smiling at his astonishment.

The great magician told him something of the way the mystic table had been built. But he darkly hinted in words the king did not wholly understand that in another day the table should be a symbol of the greatness of the reign of Uther's son.

And so indeed it happened, for, when Arthur became king, all the great knights who fought his battles gathered at the Table Round. Here they told the tales of the great deeds that cleared the bandits from the waste places and made safe the land. Here they that were all of one mind with him were given their tasks to change the old, wicked order into the new. Here they renewed the vows of that great day when they sang before the king:

"Blow trumpet, for the world is white with May!
Blow trumpet, the long night hath roll'd away!
Blow thro' the living world—'let the King reign!'

"Strike for the King and live! his knights have heard
That God hath told the King a secret word.
Fall battle-ax, and flash brand! Let the King reign!

"The King will follow Christ, and we the King,
In whom high God hath breathed a secret thing.
Fall battle-ax, and clash brand! Let the King reign!"

The Sword
Excalibur

"And near him stood the Lady of the Lake,
Who knows a subtler magic than his own—
Clothed in white samite, mystic, wonderful.
She gave the King his huge cross-hilted sword,
Whereby to drive the heathen out: a mist
Of incense curl'd about her, and her face
Wellnigh was hidden in the minster gloom;
But there was heard among the holy hymns
A voice as of the waters, for she dwells
Down in a deep—calm, whatsoever storms
May shake the world—and when the surface rolls,
Hath power to walk the waters like our Lord.
There likewise I beheld Excalibur
Before him at his crowning borne, the sword
That rose from out the bosom of the lake."

I T SOON became known all over Britain, after Arthur had drawn the sword from the stone, that the only son of Uther Pendragon had been found at last. Though some of the barons were very angry and refused at first to accept the "beardless boy," as they called him, they saw that they were wrong when the beautiful Queen Ygierne openly declared him to be the child of the dead king and herself. So Arthur was crowned with great rejoicings and feastings, and, as he sat on his throne, the assembled warriors cried that he was, in truth, their king and that they would always faithfully serve him. Then Arthur

> "in low, deep tones,
> And simple words of great authority,
> Bound them by so straight vows to his own self,
> That when they rose, knighted from kneeling, some
> Were pale as at the passing of a ghost,
> Some flush'd, and others dazed, as one who wakes
> Half-blinded at the coming of a light."

Very soon after he had become king, Arthur heard of many wrongs that had been done since the death of his father. He heard of lands that had been taken from their rightful owners and of many people who had been ill-treated in one way and another. So, having determined to be known as a great and good king, Arthur's first deed was to see that the lands were returned and the evildoers punished.

Never was there so handsome and so favored a young sovereign! Not only did all the knights and ladies of his court have the greatest affection for him, but the fairies of the forests and lakes loved him too. Had he not been given into the special care of Merlin, that master of magic who knew a hundred times as many secrets as the fairies knew themselves? Arthur's sister, too, was half a fairy, and was called "Morgain-la-Fée," which means Morgan the fairy maiden. She knew all sorts of spells, both good and bad, and could have told (though she never did) what sort of words to use if you wanted to get inside mountains or down to the bottom of deep lakes, and how to get out of such places again, which, on the whole, was almost more important than how to get in. She could read stories in the stars and tell you the wonderful enchantments that might, any moonlit night, be woven by means of a hazel wand held in a certain very secret manner. She knew exactly what kind of fern seed would make you invisible and where to find the flowers that were used for wonderful wine that smelled like primroses and wild honey and made you fall head over heels in love! There was no end to Morgain-la-Fée's magic, for, indeed, she was only a few degrees less clever than Merlin the wizard himself.

Arthur and his sister were very fond of each other; though, like a good many other brothers and sisters, they quarreled a little sometimes. It is, however, almost certain that Morgan had something to do with the way in which the young king came into possession of a second sword, much more marvelous than the one which, before he was known as Uther's son, he had pulled out of the shining white stone at Christmas time in the churchyard to give to his brother, Sir Kay.

Not very far from Arthur's castle—which was at a place called Caerleon, some distance from Tintagel—there stood a large, densely

shaded forest of tall pines and broad oaks. In
the middle of the wood was a fountain which was
always full of clear spring water. By the fountain a beautiful tent appeared one day, hung inside with satin curtains, and decorated with tassels of silver and gold. Just outside the tent a
horse in bright, rich trappings was tethered, and,
on a bough over the horse's head, hung a magnificent shield, set thickly with jewels and enam-
eled in all the colors of a peacock's tail.

As soon as this lovely tent and horse and
shield appeared by the side of the fountain, all
the passers-by knew the meaning of their coming. Some strange and powerful knight from a
distant country had taken up his post in the
middle of one of King Arthur's private forests,
and was challenging anybody and everybody to
come and turn him out. This was a thing that
happened very often in those days, and there
was never any lack of knights to answer the
challenge. In fact, the whole court was gen-
erally delighted to hear of such a stranger. It
meant honor and glory to every knight who rode
out to give the intruder battle, and great dis-
tinction to the one who succeeded in conquering
him and bringing him, a prisoner, to the throne
of the king.

The first person to come to tell Arthur about
the knight who had set up this beautiful tent by
the fountain was a very brave youth called
Griflet, who was only a page at the court of
Caerleon. He begged the king to give him the

order of knighthood that he might ride off at
once to the forest and fight with the stranger,
who, he said eagerly, was one of the strongest,
bravest, cleverest knights in the whole world.
Arthur hesitated, for he thought Griflet was too
inexperienced and young. But Merlin told him
to do as the lad asked; so the king made him a
knight as he begged, and, calling him "Sir Griflet" for the first time, made him promise to come
back to the court if he failed in the brave deed
he was so anxious to perform. Sir Griflet promised and rode off. But, in a few hours, he came
riding back again, terribly wounded and dread-
fully unhappy and disappointed. The knight by
the fountain had easily conquered him and had
thrown both him and his horse to the ground.
But instead of killing him there and then, the
stranger had, himself, dismounted and given aid
to poor Sir Griflet, telling him he was a brave
youngster and would make a fine fighter when
he was a little older. Then he had set the young
knight on his horse again, and sent him back to
the king.

When Arthur heard Sir Griflet's story, he exclaimed that the stranger was, indeed, a fine and
generous knight, and that he would himself go
to the forest and challenge him to a battle.
For, in those days, the more splendid and brave
an enemy was, the more honor there was in fighting him, even as it is today. So off rode King
Arthur on a magnificent war horse, his shield
and sword and breastplate shining, with his lord

chamberlain, mounted on another fine horse, trotting a little way behind.

On the way Merlin joined them, and walked by the king's stirrup, saying he thought he might be wanted before the day was over. As he and Arthur talked together, they came in sight of the richly colored tent, with the strange knight, dressed in all his bright armor, standing by the side of the tree where his shield was hanging, its jewels and enamel gleaming in the shade of the boughs. When he saw another knight riding in the forest, he stepped forward and stood, very proud and erect, barring the way that led onward through the wood.

"How now!" cried Arthur. "Then no one may pass this way without a fight?"

"That is so," answered the knight, in a bold and haughty manner. "Are you ready?"

"Quite ready!" replied Arthur joyfully. "Mount your horse, and we will see which of us is the better knight."

So the stranger leaped upon his horse, and, with sword and spear, king and knight sprang toward each other to do battle. Such a crash rang through the forest as they met! If you heard it today you would think some dreadful accident had happened! But the crash was only the noise of the king's spear striking the shield of the knight, and the knight's spear striking the shield of the king. And so vigorously did each strike that both the spears were shivered into a thousand pieces.

Guinevere turned from her father to the stranger knight.

Then the lord chamberlain rode up with two new, unbroken spears, and the two brave warriors met again with even a louder crash than before. Again each spear was shattered to bits. By this time, both king and knight were hot with battle, and, springing from their horses, they rushed at each other on foot, brandishing their sharp, shining swords. Over and over again they struck, one at the other, each trying to strike the conquering blow. At last the stranger knight drew back for a moment, and King Arthur, thinking he was exhausted, leaped toward him, but the other swung his sword suddenly high above his head, and brought it with all his force against the king's sword as Arthur made his spring. So violent was the knight's great blow that it cut right through the sword of the king, who was left with only the jagged handle in his grasp.

Then Arthur threw away the handle, and rushed at the knight with his mailed gloves. So they fought again, rocking and swaying together like two mighty wrestlers. But, at last, King Arthur was thrown to the ground, and lay senseless among the bruised ferns and crushed wild flowers of the forest floor.

The stranger knight lifted high his own unbroken sword, whether or not to strike the fainting king none ever knew, for Merlin, who had been watching, sprang forward and waved his wizard's wand. The knight slipped slowly to the ground, and lay beside the king in a deep sleep; while Merlin lifted Arthur, and set him, only half conscious, on the stranger's horse.

The king, pale and exhausted, looked down on the knight as Merlin led the horse away. "Oh, Merlin, Merlin!" he cried. "You have killed the finest knight that ever did battle against a king!" "Not so!" answered Merlin. "He is only asleep, and it is a good thing for you he is not awake! But come! You must have another sword to make up for the one that has been broken in the fight!"

So on they went through the trees, Merlin still leading the horse. Presently they came to a big open space in the forest, and there, in the afternoon sunlight, glimmered the wide waters of a mysterious lake. Nothing was in sight— no cottages, no castles, no people, no wild foxes or deer. But out in the middle of the lake a white hand and arm were stretched out from the water, as motionless as if they were carved in ivory. A long sleeve of pearly satin was folded about the arm, and the slender hand held the most beautiful jeweled sword that Arthur had ever seen.

As the king looked, amazed, he saw a golden-haired fairy maiden in a silver gown walking on the green water just as a pretty girl might trip across a green meadow. She came stepping daintily toward them, and Arthur asked Merlin who she was. "She is Nimue, the Lady of the Lake," said Merlin, "and if you ask her very

courteously, she will tell you how to get the
sword." So, when the Lady of the Lake set her
pretty little foot on the shore, Arthur went toward her and, bowing very low, asked her to tell
him how he might get the sword.

Then the maiden smiled and showed him a
fairy barge, snugly hidden among the reeds and
rushes. She told him he had but to get into the
barge, row himself into the middle of the lake,
and take the sword out of the fair white hand
which held it. "And as my reward for telling
you this," said she, "one day I shall come to the
court and claim a favor from you!" Then she
disappeared, and Arthur and Merlin, springing
into the barge, rowed out into the middle of the
lake as fast as they could.

All this time the hand and arm that held the
sword had remained quite still. How strange
they looked, rising so mysteriously from the
quiet, glimmering water! How Arthur mar-
veled, as he drew nearer and nearer, at the slim
wrist and the delicate fingers of that white,
strange hand! What lady or fairy could it be
who lived under the waves of that wonderful
mere and was offering this beautiful jeweled gift
to a human king?

The barge drew close up to the motionless
arm, and Arthur, leaning over the side, put out
his hand. Very gently and carefully he drew
the shining sword from the fairy fingers. As
soon as he touched the sword they released their
clasp, and the arm sank slowly, slowly down into

the lake. The ripples closed over it with a little murmur, and it was gone.

And Arthur, when he examined the sword, saw that on one side of the blade the words "Take me" were engraved, and that on the other side appeared the legend "Cast me away." When he had read these words he became very sad, but Merlin said, "Take the sword and make good use of it, for the time when you will have to cast it away is very far off."

Then Merlin rowed the barge back again to the rocky, reedy bank of the lake. The lady who had told them to take the sword was nowhere to be seen. She had disappeared entirely, and had left not so much as a glimmer of her silver gown or a gleam of her golden hair among the dark pines that grew close down to the water's edge.

Arthur and Merlin stepped out of the barge, and Arthur fastened the fairy sword to his side. Then Merlin, who had read all about it in one of his fairy books, told him that the sword was called "Excalibur," and that it was just as precious and wonderful as the Round Table itself. The wizard told the king, too, the name of the stranger knight, which was Pellinore, and said that he, also, was a great king. But when Arthur wanted to go and finish the battle with Pellinore —now that he was armed with a fairy sword— Merlin said that he had fought quite enough for one day. So he and the king rode back to Caerleon with Excalibur hanging by Arthur's side;

while King Pellinore awoke quietly from his enchanted sleep and went to rest in his tent, hung
with silken curtains and golden tassels, that he
had set up by the side of the fern-fringed fountain, in the shade of the forest trees.

Guinevere

"Leodogran, the king of Cameliard,
Had one fair daughter, and none other child;
And she was fairest of all flesh on earth,
Guinevere, and in her his one delight."

KING LEODOGRAN, as you know, was an old friend of King Uther Pendragon, who had given into his charge Merlin's wonderful Round Table where seats could be found for two hundred and fifty knights. This Round Table was kept in the banqueting hall of Leodogran's big stone castle at Cameliard. All the knights who feasted there were under a vow; and the words of this vow were some of the noblest words that have ever been spoken in the history of the world. Besides the Round Table, Leodogran's castle held another great treasure —his only daughter, Guinevere, the most beautiful and most gracious maiden in the whole, wide earth.

Guinevere flitted about the castle almost like a fairy princess, so golden was her hair, so blue were her eyes, so peach pink her delicately rounded cheeks. Sometimes she sang to herself softly, in the great hall; sometimes she sat in her bedroom window, doing embroidery; sometimes she went to and fro among her maidens, overseeing them as they spun linen thread upon their pretty spinning wheels, or wove the same thread into shining damask on their dainty looms. When her father's step was heard on the flags of the stone floors, Guinevere would lay everything aside and hasten to meet him. If he were tired and battle-worn—as often, indeed, she found him—she would bring him cool, clear water in a silver basin, place his hands in it, and dry them herself with a fine towel, before offering him a crystal goblet brimming with red wine to drink. Leodogran would gladly have died in the defense of his daughter Guinevere, though he was silent and almost cold to her, and sometimes, even, very strict and stern.

One morning, the King of Cameliard, who had been away for some days, came galloping back to the castle on his war horse and cried to the servants to let down the portcullis, or great entrance door, to raise the bridge over the moat, and to prepare for a siege. His enemies were riding in hundreds over the surrounding hills. The Knights of the Round Table came hurrying into the great hall, their pages running after them to buckle on their masters' armor as fast as they could. But instead of a page, Leodogran was waited upon by his own daughter, the Princess Guinevere, who brought him his helmet, breastplate, sword, and shield. Praying to heaven to protect him, she watched the king ride out of the courtyard at the head of his noble knights. Then she, herself, looked after the preparations for the siege of the castle before, running lightly up the winding stone stairs, she took up her stand by the window of a high tower from which she could watch the battle.

What a clash of armies she saw outside! What waving of banners, galloping and rearing of horses, cries of triumph or despair! Here, there, and everywhere flashed Leodogran in his bright armor, supported always by the knights of the Round Table. For long they held their own, but by and by Princess Guinevere, gazing always from the window, felt her heart shaken with sudden fear. She saw the knights pressed hard on every side by an army stronger in numbers than themselves. They fought fiercely and magnificently, but they were being driven back toward the castle walls. Would they be able to drive away these eager and terrible regiments of foes? Or would they be forced to yield and give Cameliard into the hands of the enemy?

Princess Guinevere tried hard to keep up a good heart, but, when the tide of battle seemed to have turned against her father, the numbness of dismay seized her. Then, suddenly, she heard a shout of encouragement and triumph. Down

among her father's foes came riding an unknown
knight, the noblest in bearing, most beautiful in
face, and brightest in armor, that the princess
had ever seen. Above his head floated a banner
which displayed a dragon wrought in burnished
gold! In his hand flashed a sword of gleaming
steel, its handle studded with diamonds, rubies,
and pearls. Who was he, and whence could he
have come?

Guinevere leaned far out of the casement,
joyful and reassured, for the tide of battle immediately turned. In and out, backward and
forward, glittered the golden sign of the dragon,
while the strange knight's sword swept through
the enemy like an avenging flame. Whoever was
touched by this sword, however lightly, fell from
his horse to the ground. Its owner seemed to
be everywhere at once. He had slain hundreds
of Leodogran's enemies, when, as if he had
dropped from the sky, an old man appeared at
his side, seized the bridle, and threw his war
horse back upon its haunches.

"Enough!" cried this old man—who had
come from no one knew where—"enough! Do
you not see that the battle is won? The whole
enemy army is in flight!"

Then the stranger knight paused and saw,
indeed, a confused mass of men and horses riding fast for the distant hills. He bowed his head
and slowly slid his sword into its sheath. Then
up rode King Leodogran, grim, blood-stained,
and weary, and bent low in his saddle to the

young, brave stranger who had saved his castle
and all that was in it.

"Beautiful and courageous knight!" said
Leodogran. "How can I thank you? Come—
follow me into my castle. I do not know who
you are, but you have saved my home for me,
and anything or everything in it is yours for
the asking."

The knight also bent low in his saddle, for the
knights of those days were always very dignified
and very courteous. Then the big portcullis was
raised again, and the bridge lowered over the
moat. Two and two, kings and knights, they
all rode into the courtyard of the castle, and the
clatter of the horses' feet reached Princess Guinevere as she came hurrying down from the window of the high tower.

How busy everybody in the castle was, to be
sure! Pages, with big baskets on their arms,
were strewing the floors with bright fresh
rushes, mingled with wild flowers. Cooks, in
the kitchen, were roasting and stewing and bak-
ing with all their might. Delighted, smiling
maidens were pouring cool, scented water into
basins, taking clean white towels out of the
presses, and bringing soft, rich robes into the
big hall, ready to lay on the knights' shoulders
when the pages had taken off the stained and
heavy armor in which these brave gentlemen
had fought.

King Leodogran led the stranger knight to
the seat of honor and bade him rest. As the

tired soldier sank down upon a couch all clean
and fresh with piles of sweet-smelling rushes,
he saw a lovely lady coming quickly forward
from among the serving maidens who were
waiting on the knights of the Round Table. To
the stranger knight, she seemed like a beautiful
picture as she came forward, cautiously bearing
a silver basin and snow-white towel, while a
truant ray of sunlight lay on her golden headdress and dainty silken gown. It was the Princess
Guinevere, hastening to wait, courteously and
lovingly, on her father, the king.

But, as she curtsied deeply to him, he waved
her from him and pointed to his guest, who was
watching eagerly from his couch of green
rushes. "Wait, first, on the stranger knight,"
said Leodogran. "Had it not been for his help,
the castle of Cameliard would have fallen."

So Guinevere turned from her father to the
stranger knight. And, the moment the eyes of the
knight and the maiden met, the two fell in love!

How wonderful it seemed to both! The soldier in his armor looked adoringly at the sweet
face under the golden headdress, the long hair,
no less golden, which fell in two plaits to the
very hem of this fair lady's gown. Guinevere,
for her part, hardly lifted her shy blue eyes from
the ground as she helped the stranger take off
his breastplate, laid a rich satin cloak on his
shoulders, offered him the water and the towel,
and called to a servant to bring a refreshing
drink. The old man, who had entered the castle

with the knights, smiled as he watched them, and, drawing near to Leodogran, pointed out the pretty sight.

"You offered anything your castle held, to your deliverer," said he. "I think I know what gift your visitor will be asking soon!"

King Leodogran started and looked rather dismayed.

"Who is he?" he asked. "And who, old man, are you?"

The king stared very closely at his unknown visitor, who only shook his head.

"No matter—no matter!" said he. "But what of your promise to give the knight anything he asks?"

"My promise shall be kept," said Leodogran proudly. And the old man smiled again as he stepped away.

Then everyone in the hall began to move toward the banqueting room, and the two hundred and fifty knights took their places at the Round Table, which was spread for a feast. King Leodogran stood watching them, and the stranger knight stepped forward and joined him, looking at him very earnestly indeed.

"Good and great King," said he, "I am from a distant court, and do not know your customs here. What is this Round Table and who are these knights who have taken their places about it?"

Leodogran answered gravely. "Brave stranger," he said, "that Round Table was left in my

charge by a great king—Uther Pendragon himself. Whoever takes his place at it must share in
a noble vow. Will you sit among my two hundred
and fifty knights? Will you join in the words
of the vow?"

The knight's face had become very bright
and eager when he heard the name of Uther
Pendragon. He looked to the right and saw the
old man's eyes fixed earnestly upon him; he
glanced to the left and met the shy, gentle gaze
of beautiful Guinevere. Then he made a quick
step forward and took his seat at the table
among the two hundred and fifty knights.

"Will you admit me to your fellowship?" he
cried in a piercing voice. "Will you let me hear
and share the words of your vow?"

Then, as one, the two hundred and fifty
knights sprang to their feet, and two hundred
and fifty voices rang out lustily in the great
vow:

"To right the wrong, to punish the guilty, to
feed the hungry, to help the feeble, to obey the
law, and never to turn away from a woman in
distress; this is the high and solemn vow of the
Knights of the Round Table!"

The sound of voices ceased, and everyone
turned to the stranger, who had drawn his
sword, and was holding it on high. Word for
word, he repeated the vow in a ringing voice,
and then thrust his sword back into the scabbard, looking, with his whole heart in his eyes,
at Princess Guinevere.

Leodogran stepped forward and held up his hand for silence.

"Sir Knight," he said, "who are you?"

With a triumphant smile, the stranger answered him, "I am Arthur, King of Britain, and proud so to be, but far, far prouder to have become a Knight of the Round Table——"

He paused for a moment, then moved swiftly forward and knelt on one knee before Guinevere, as he finished speaking. "And proudest of all, King Leodogran, to put my sword, my spear, my life, at the service of this fair and gentle lady!"

Then the old man came toward them, and King Leodogran knew him to be Merlin, the great magician. Merlin, glancing toward Arthur, took Guinevere's hand and laid it on her father's palm; Leodogran with a smile placed it in Arthur's ready clasp, and, raising him to his feet, bent very low before him.

"My liege and lord," said he, "I would have given my daughter gladly to the knight who saved Cameliard. How much more joyfully I give her to Arthur, son of Uther Pendragon, King of Britain, and Knight of the Round Table!"

The Seat
Perilous

"This is the siege of Galahad."

ONE spring morning the sun rose bright and beautiful over the high towers of Camelot. The birds were singing among the apple blooms; the oak trees were shaking out their little tufts of greeny gold; the May blossoms were nodding their heads among the long grass all spangled with dew. Camelot was hung with banners and flags; its doors were decorated with silken curtains; and its pathways were arched with rainbows of flowers. Magnificent tapestries adorned the walls; fresh rushes, mixed with garlands, covered the stone floors. Servants were hastening here and there with silver dishes containing cakes and fruit and honey, and golden goblets and wine. For King Arthur's wedding day was close at hand, and Guinevere was on her way to Camelot with a train of ladies-in-waiting and a bodyguard of

knights. They were bringing, too, the Round
Table that had been made by Merlin in imitation
of the Silver Table brought so long ago, by Joseph and the Rich Fisher, to the country of West-
over-the-Sea.

At this Round Table, as you know, the young
king had taken his knightly vow. How glad he
was to think that it was to stand under the roof
of Camelot, and that, sitting all about it, his fellow knights would join in his wedding break-
fast. He stood with Merlin in the great gateway
of his royal castle, dressed in armor that shone
like gold. All about him were his faithful courtiers waiting to greet the strangers who were
coming from the court of Leodogran. The great
company of the Round Table was to be com-
pleted today. Many knights had made the vow
in times gone by; some had failed to keep it,
and some had been killed in battle. But today,
the day before Arthur's wedding, every seat was
to be filled.

This was the king's purpose, as he waited at
the entrance of his castle in his armor of gold.
Presently, from the distance came the murmur
of a crowd, the tramping of horses' feet, and the
roll of wheels. Over the hills toward Camelot
poured the glittering procession of the royal
bride—banners waving, and minstrels singing
stirring and noble songs. It was a magnificent
sight, and no less magnificent was the sight that
was waiting for the strangers in King Arthur's
own splendid court.

Arthur's heart was beating fast with excitement and joy as the procession came along the
meadow until it halted at the great castle gates.
He moved forward and bent very, very low. For,
on the leading horse, he saw his lovely lady
Guinevere, riding in royal dignity, a rich hood
hiding her beautiful golden hair and an embroidered and jeweled cloak hanging from her slender shoulders. Close behind her rode her pages,
ready to answer any call that she might give.
Then came her ladies-in-waiting, each with a
handsome knight in attendance. In the very
midst of the procession marched a tall old man
in white, crowned with mistletoe and singing
songs to the sound of a harp that he held in his
hands, while a number of men followed just
behind carrying the Round Table!

King Arthur stepped forward and lifted
Guinevere from her horse. Who knows what
fond words he whispered to her before he set
her on the ground? Then he took her hand and
led her forward, across the courtyard, between
rows of smiling, bowing attendants, right into
the castle of Camelot, with the knights and
ladies who had come with her from her father's
court walking two and two behind.

A beautiful throne had been set high on a
dais for the princess, and Arthur led her up to
it and saw her seat herself, before he turned to
welcome the noble company who followed. He
bowed over the hands of the fair ladies, and all
the knights bent, with stately courtesy, in greet-

ing. The Round Table was brought in and put
in the very middle of the hall. Arthur drew near
and watched, while his servants placed the seats
about it; and, when they had set as many as it
would hold, the king called to all the knights who
belonged to the fellowship of the Round Table
to gather around.

From among the brilliant company in the
hall, a hundred knights stepped forward, all of
whom had come with Princess Guinevere from
the court of her father, King Leodogran. As
they approached the Round Table, Arthur
counted them over, one by one. When the hundred were complete, the king bowed to them once
more. Then he turned to Merlin, who again stood
beside him. Merlin took a roll of parchment,
blazoned with many a noble coat of arms, from
beneath his wizard's robe and began to read
aloud from it.

He was reading the names of those among
Arthur's own knights who had, for their courage
and their goodness, their truth, charity, and up-
rightness, been considered worthy to join the
noble fellowship of the Round Table. Some were
old and scarred with battle; some were middle-
aged; some were quite young, keen, and vigorous to fight for honor and for the king. When
the names rang down the hall they stepped forward, one by one. Bowing to Princess Guinevere
as they passed the high dais, and to King Arthur
as they came to where he stood, they joined the
hundred knights from the court of King Leodo-

gran. Then the chief butler came forward with
a great jeweled goblet in his hand, followed by
two pages carrying golden jugs. The knights
and the king took their seats in the great carved
chairs about the table; the goblet was filled, and,
passing the jeweled cup from hand to hand,
everybody drank to the fellowship of knights
good and brave and true—the great Fellowship
of the Round Table.

All this time Guinevere watched, smiling and
gracious, from her throne on the high dais. Her
ladies-in-waiting were gathered about her, form-
ing in their gay dresses a setting of colorful
posies for her, the bright, central flower. The
knights looked at each other, and at the king,
as they drank from the glittering cup. They all
rose to their feet and looked toward their future
queen on her throne in the midst of them as, at
a sign from Arthur, their voices rang out, loud
and joyful and brave, in the words of the great
vow.

The sound died away, and it was now the
Princess Guinevere's turn to rise to her feet,
sweet, and fair, and royal among them all. How
proud and happy the king must have felt when
he saw his lady standing among these bright
and gallant gentlemen, accepting their promise
of chivalry with so delicate a grace! Her hair
shone in the light that fell from the high windows; her silk gown swept softly to her little
slippered feet. She curtsied very low to them
all, and waved her pretty, white hands. Then

she sat down again among her ladies; and, one by one, the knights of the Round Table stepped gravely forward and, kneeling on one knee before Arthur, took the oath of loyalty to the king.

Merlin stood by, his scroll of parchment again rolled up neatly in his hand. As each knight made his vow, the wizard bent his grave, wise head. But, constantly, he was gazing at the Round Table. He seemed, as if in a dream, to see the vision of the Silver Table, and Joseph, and the Rich Fisher, and the Shining Cup that was called the Holy Grail.

Then, while he looked at the Round Table, he saw a mysterious thing happen. On all the seats that were placed about it letters of gold began to appear. They looked as if they were being written by invisible fingers holding an invisible pen. As Merlin watched, these letters grew bigger and brighter, so that they could be seen from quite a long way off. The old magician moved forward to read them the more clearly; and when he stood quite close to the table, the wonder on his face changed into great gladness for he knew that good spirits were in the banqueting hall and that they had come from that mysterious distant Fairyland where the Silver Table and the Shining Cup had been hidden so many, many years ago.

For what do you think had been written in each seat by the invisible fingers that held the invisible pen? No less than the name of the knight who had just risen from it to do homage to King Arthur, chief of them all. It was a sure sign to Merlin that the Round Table had been made, by his own hands, for these very knights, and that their names were written also about the Silver Table which had been lost to men. He called to the king and to the knights to come and read. They all gathered around; amazed, and spelled out the letters of their names; and then they took their places, shoulder to shoulder and hand to hand. But, even as they did so, they saw that not every seat was filled. Two of them, one on Arthur's right hand, the other on his left, were still empty and unnamed.

Then King Arthur was very much grieved and disappointed, for he had hoped that today the Fellowship of the Round Table would be quite complete. But Merlin had, in an instant, seen into the future, and he knew the secret of those two empty seats. He laid his hand on the King's shoulder and consoled him.

"Be patient," said the magician, "be patient! In one empty seat you will very soon see somebody whom you know and admire already, though, just now, I shall not tell you who he is! In the other, the Seat Perilous, no knight may sit today, nor tomorrow, nor for many years to come. And woe betide any knight who thinks that he may take his place at the Round Table in that place without a right! Look! See what dread legend is written there instead of a name!"

Arthur looked, and lo! he saw letters appear about the second empty seat, written, not in gold, but in flame! Marveling, he read the words,

I am the Seat Perilous.

Even as he finished reading the words, they faded away. But all the knights and all the ladies and Princess Guinevere herself, had seen the letters of flame. And, throughout the court, ran the murmur of the words, "That empty seat is the Seat Perilous, and no knight may sit in it today, nor tomorrow, nor for many years to come!"

A Hunt in
Fairyland

"Right so as they sat there came running in a white hart into
the hall, and a white brachet next him, and thirty couple of
black running hounds came after with great cry."

KING ARTHUR and Princess Guinevere
were married with great rejoicing, and
all the barons and baronesses, the dukes and
duchesses of the country, came to the wedding.
Such a banquet there was at Camelot! Such
songs and dances and tournaments! The whole
neighborhood seemed to ring with the mirth of
it; with the shouts and laughter and delicate
music of a hundred harps. Every evening the
king and queen sat at the windows of the castle,
watching processions of knights, with torches,
winding in and out among the trees. Every
morning the radiant pair came out together,
smiling and beautiful, to walk or ride across the
meadow so that the whole world might see them.
The queen moved along daintily and silently, but
the king was always watchful and alert, ready

to hear grievances or to grant favors; ready even
to give the order of knighthood to the poor sons
of laborers and cowherds, if they could prove to
him that they were as noble and valiant at heart
as any gentleman of the land. And both nobles
and commons bowed low, not from fear but from
love, as they passed.

But a day came when Merlin told Arthur that
the merriment and feasting must pause for a
time, and that the king must meet his knights in
sober and earnest talk, seated at the Round
Table. So Queen Guinevere and all the ladies of
the court swept and rustled away in a stately
procession to the women's quarters in the castle,
while the king and the knights sat down at the
Round Table, and passed the cup of fellowship
from hand to hand. Then Merlin said that today
the empty seat at the king's left hand was to be
filled—not the Seat Perilous, but the other place
that had been left without a name. Everybody
wondered who the chosen knight could be; and
they all stood up and waited as the great wizard
went out of the door of the banqueting hall to
bring in the newcomer, and to present him to
the king.

After a minute or two the sound of a galloping horse was heard through the window—a
powerful, swift horse which came, with thunder-
ing hoofs, over the drawbridge of the moat. A
knight's armor clashed in the courtyard; a
knight's small silken banner fluttered against
the casement. Merlin's voice spoke a greeting,

and deep, full, gay tones echoed in reply. Down
the corridor tramped the heavy feet of the stranger, and in the doorway his form showed, tall
and broad. Merlin took his hand and led him
forward, and King Arthur gave a cry of amazement; for it was none other than King Pellinore,
the knight who had set up his tent by the side
of the woodland fountain, and who had been left
lying in an enchanted sleep the last time that
Arthur had seen him!

But King Arthur was pleased—oh, very
pleased indeed! He bore the other king no ill
will for having broken his own royal sword—
and very nearly his own royal head as well—in
their mighty battle among the forest trees. Stepping forward, he greeted his old enemy warmly,
declaring that he was a right goodly and noble
knight, worthy to become a member of the
Round Table. Pellinore said, in reply, that he
was proud of many things in his life, but never
prouder than at this moment, when he stood in
the halls of Camelot and received the greeting
of Camelot's king. Then he bent on one knee
before Arthur, and took the oath of fealty; and
Arthur himself raised him up, and placed him
in the seat at the left-hand side, while the jeweled cup was passed round again, and all the
other knights drank joyfully to Pellinore, the
latest, and almost the finest, comer to the Round
Table.

And now Merlin made a sign to Arthur, and
the king sprang to his feet and drew his sword

from his scabbard. As one, the other swords flashed. There was a moment's pause, and then all the brave voices rang out together. Standing side by side, shoulder to shoulder, their unsheathed swords glittering, their heads erect, the knights of the Round Table thundered out the words of the vow.

The sound of the vow was still in the air, and not one of the company had sheathed his sword, when a great commotion arose under the windows of the castle! Hounds were baying, horns were blowing, and a little dog seemed to be barking with all its might! A long, long way off, horses might be heard galloping, as well. But nobody could be quite sure of that, because, as they all stared at each other in great astonishment, the door of the banqueting hall suddenly burst open, and a great pure-white stag, with branching horns and eyes like balls of flame, bounded into the room, its hoofs, which seemed to be made of silver, flashing and ringing among the green rushes on the stone flags of the floor.

No sooner had it leaped through the doorway than everybody saw that the little white dog, which had been making such a noise outside, was hard on the heels of this beautiful and mysterious deer. And, following instantly, came a pack of thirty couples of great, black hounds in full cry after the snow-white stag. But of followers and huntsmen there was not a sign. Only the sound of fairy horns blowing in the air, and the galloping of unseen horses very far away.

Round the big banqueting hall swept this strange hunt, which was in very truth a hunt from Fairyland. Just as the great white stag reached the place where a young, handsome knight was sitting, the little dog sprang up at it, so that the big beautiful creature leaped almost over the young knight's head. This knight was called Sir Gawaine, and the stag knocked him from his feet in its flight from the little dog and the baying pack of hounds. Such a noise there was in the banqueting hall! Sir Gawaine sprang up, quite bewitched, and, catching up the little dog, joined the hunt, not knowing that it was a fairy hunt and would lead him no one could tell whither! Away he ran out of the room and out of the castle, and, putting the little dog on his horse, just as huntsmen always did, went galloping off after the snow-white stag, with the thirty couples of coal-black hounds racing alongside. But no sooner was he gone out of the door than a beautiful maiden, on a prancing white pony, came in at another door and rode down to the middle of the hall. Pulling up her dainty steed, she called to King Arthur to go after Sir Gawaine and to bring back the little fairy dog which he had stolen!

"The little dog is mine!" cried this beautiful unknown lady. "The knight had no business to take it away! Remember the vow, King Arthur, remember the vow! I am a lady in distress, and, as such, you have sworn an oath to help me!"

King Arthur sat silent, his hand on his
sword, and his eyes cast down. The vow had
seemed to him such a beautiful, serious thing,
and he could not believe that it had anything to
do with this wild fairy hunt, and this strange
fairy lady, who certainly was not made of flesh
and blood, but belonged to some enchanted forest a very long way off. He heard the noise of
the black hounds and of Sir Gawaine's horse
and of the little mysterious elfin dog fade in the
distance among the faintly blowing horns of the
invisible company, and he had not the slightest
wish to go after them. He wanted to stay quietly
in his royal castle with his beautiful royal bride.

As he hesitated, another startling and quite
unexpected visitor came noisily in through the
wide-open door. This time it was a strange,
shadowy knight almost as large as a giant,
dressed in black armor, and riding a huge black
horse. He trotted up to the lady, and, without
a word to anybody, seized her pretty white pony
by the bridle. Then he wheeled his horse about
and rode quickly out of the door again, leading
the lady's pony, and taking no notice of her cries
and tears. It all happened so quickly that not a
single knight of the Round Table had time
to spring to the lady's rescue, nor even to see
the face of the shadowy knight in the black
armor.

As they all stood breathless and amazed,
King Arthur suddenly found his voice, and cried
aloud, in ringing tones, to Merlin, the magician:

"Tell me, O great wizard," he cried, "what is the meaning of all this magic? Whence did the fairy stag, and the fairy hounds, and the fairy lady, and the shadowy black knight come? Was it not from your own Enchanted Forest where stands the Perilous Castle in the middle of the Valley of No Return?"

Merlin, whose face had been hidden under his magician's hood, suddenly flung away the covering. Everybody saw him, for a moment, as an old man with a long white beard, wearing a crown of mistletoe. But even as they looked his face changed. He seemed young and very beautiful, and the crown of mistletoe became a laurel wreath on his hair, which was golden and like a boy's. His voice, when he answered Arthur, somehow reminded the king of the invisible fairy horns which they had all heard and which, no doubt, had called Sir Gawaine to the elfin hunt after them.

"And what if the hunt is only a fairy hunt and the lady only a fairy lady?" cried Merlin, in this new mysterious silvery tone of voice. "Are you not brave enough to follow them into Fairyland? Is all your life going to be spent in royal castles, eating and drinking at rich banquets, listening to the music of golden harps, and meeting other knights in mock battles, with swords and shields? Do you not know what high adventure means? If not, I can soon tell you! It means the adventure of bright dreams, and of lovely visions, and of things that are only very dimly seen and heard. Follow the fairy hunt, good King Arthur! Pursue the vision of the snow-white stag, and the sweet sorrowful lady, and the dark knight! What if she has only asked you to bring back her little white dog? What if you think it is all magic mixed with folly, and you would be better staying quietly at home? Have the kingly courage to take horse and to follow Sir Gawaine into Fairyland—to storm the doors of the Castle Perilous and to brave the darkness of the Valley of No Return!"

Then Arthur drew himself erect, and King Pellinore sprang to his feet at the king's right hand. "I, too, am a king," cried Pellinore. "I, too, am of royal blood! It is for kings to lead the way into the mysterious places of which the great wizard has spoken. Come, King Arthur! Together we will set off on this high adventure!"

"You say well!" cried Merlin. "You say well! You have your own good sword, King Pellinore! You have used it well and strongly more than once. Use it well and strongly again! And for you, my own great sovereign, my dearly loved Arthur, you have Excalibur! Excalibur that you took from the hand that held it high above the enchanted lake! Carry Excalibur with you, and use it, always, to defend the right. Then you need not fear the places of dark spirits and of old unhappy witcheries! Forward, forward, both of you! Go, like brave and chivalrous kings, into Fairyland! What you will see and find there will be your great and inestimable reward!"

Merlin finished speaking, and folded his hood once more about his face and hair. King Arthur and King Pellinore went out of the banqueting hall and sprang each upon his own war horse. Then off they went, side by side, after the fairy hunt, while Merlin, hidden in his hood, passed away from the sight of the knights of the Round Table. Where he went none of them knew: very likely back to his own home in the forest—the forest in which he had once seen the vision of Joseph and the Rich Fisher and the Holy Grail.

Merlin knew that one day King Arthur and King Pellinore and all the knights of the Round Table would see the vision, too; but that this would be only when they had passed through the dangers of the Enchanted Forest and stormed the Castle Perilous, and had gone, without losing themselves entirely, through the valley that was called the Valley of No Return.

The Rescue
of Nimue

"O hark, O hear! how thin and clear,
 And thinner, clearer, farther going!
O sweet and far from cliff and scar
 The horns of Elfland faintly blowing!"

KING PELLINORE, that huge knight who once nearly killed King Arthur and then took a place at the Round Table and made the great vow, had many adventures in his day, but the one you are going to hear about was the greatest of all. You remember that he had galloped off at full speed after the fairy hunt. As he galloped he swore to himself that he would save the pretty, weeping lady who had been carried off by the Black Knight and would bring her back in safety from the Enchanted Forest. He had become separated from King Arthur, and was now quite alone among the trees of this strange place; but, just in front of him, he could still hear the baying and yelping of the sixty coal-black hounds.

82

He rode on as fast as he could, and then
something happened that would have amazed
another knight, but did not surprise King Pellinore at all because he had known such a thing
to happen before. The baying of the hounds
suddenly became muffled and strange, as if they
had disappeared inside a cave. The king turned
the corner, and there, in front of him, stood a
great beast that was not like a lion nor a bear
nor even a dragon nor anything in the world
except itself. It stood and glared at him, before
turning round and lumbering away, crashing
through the undergrowth with as much noise as
a hippopotamus would have made. And through
the mouth of the beast there still came the muffled baying of the hounds. This strange monster had swallowed them all, but they seemed
still to be hunting the fairy stag in the very
middle of the beast's inside!

King Pellinore gave a great shout, for he
had been hunting this beast all his life and knew
that he would probably go on hunting it until
he died and never be able to kill it, after all!
But, meanwhile, he followed it hard through
bush and brier, often losing sight of it, but always hearing the strange muffled music of the
fairy hounds. At last the beast disappeared al-
together, and he saw a lady sitting by a fountain
who showed him the path that he must take
through the Enchanted Forest and told him that
already the Black Knight and the pretty, weeping maiden had gone that way. So then King

Pellinore knew that, in following the beast, he had come in the right direction for the fulfilment of his vow.

He heard the hounds still baying, but a long, long way off, as he hurried down the path shown him by the lady. In a very few minutes he reached a clearing in the wood where two beautiful tents, one blue and one crimson, were set up opposite each other in the flickering lights and shadows of the trees. At the door of one of these tents stood the maiden he had come to save; and on the trodden grass in the middle of the clearing the Black Knight, on the black horse, was doing battle with sword and shield against another knight who seemed almost as big and strong as his enemy.

King Pellinore poised his spear in his raised hand and, galloping forward, drove his way between them. "How, now?" he cried. "How is this? Who are you both, that you fight in this way for the lady yonder, who belongs to neither of you, but came, of her own will, to ask the protection of King Arthur?"

The Black Knight had pulled his great horse on to its haunches, but he shouted back at King Pellinore, whom he did not know as one of the knights of the Round Table.

"The lady is mine!" cried the Black Knight shaking his lance. "This foolish fellow, here, is trying to steal her from me. But she is mine! I fought King Arthur for her, and I conquered him!"

*Then the Black Knight rushed upon King Pellinore and they fought
until the forest rang with the noise.*

"That is not true!" shouted King Pellinore
—and his voice in its anger rang all through the
forest—"I was there and I saw it all! You carried the lady away before a single knight of the
Round Table had time to spring to arms and do
battle for her. But every man of Arthur's court
knows you have no right to her! I have followed
the coal-black hounds, and the beast which swallowed the hounds, all the way through this Enchanted Forest to take the lady back again!
Come! Meet me here in this open space of
grass, and we will soon see which is the better
man."

Then the Black Knight rushed upon King
Pellinore, and with their swords and shields and
spears they fought until the forest rang with the
noise. But the king was soon the conqueror. He
killed the Black Knight's horse, and, when he
saw his enemy lying on the crushed turf, he also
sprang to the ground, to finish the fight fairly
on foot. And finish it he did, for he cut off the
wicked Black Knight's head.

Then the other knight, who had watched the
battle from a little distance, came forward gladly, and told King Pellinore to take the lady back
to Arthur's court. "I was but trying to save her
from the Black Knight," he said. "I knew that
he had no right to her!" And he brought out a
fresh, strong horse that had been tethered to a
tree, and put King Pellinore's saddle and bridle
upon it and said he would care for the tired, hot
horse which had been in the battle. Then he

went up to the door of the tent, and giving his hand to the lady led her forward.

The lady had stopped crying now, and had let down her long veil and wound her hood about her head, so that King Pellinore could not see her face. He lifted her into the saddle before springing up in front of her, and as she lay for an instant in his powerful arms there seemed to rise to his nostrils the perfume of wild roses and violets washed in dew. How lightly she seemed to sit behind him, too! His big horse took no count of her extra weight as it trotted off through the trees, where the night shadows were gathering and the stars already twinkling high up above the boughs.

On and on rode King Pellinore and the lady until it was quite dark. Then he stopped his horse, and lifted her down, and guarded her while she slept under the trees. He was almost surprised to see in the morning that she was still there, because he guessed she was more than half a fairy and unlike an ordinary mortal. When they rode on again, and passed out of the Enchanted Forest, he wondered if she would take wing, like a moth or a butterfly, and remain behind! But she did not, and when the sun was high in the sky both king and lady rode safely into the courtyard of the castle at Camelot.

Then King Arthur and Sir Gawaine (who having soon lost the sound of the fairy hunt, had returned without encountering any adventures

worth recording), and all the rest came out to
meet them, and welcomed the lady right gladly,
and gave praise and honor to King Pellinore.
But the lady was still veiled, and, at last, King
Arthur turned to her with courtesy.

"You will find shelter and happiness forever
at my court," said he. "The knights of the
Round Table will be at your service, always—
ready to protect you, and never failing to honor
you. But you came and went almost as swiftly,
and with as much surprise to us, as the fairy
hunt itself—to which, somehow, I think you half
belong. Will you, then, let us now see your face?"

Then the lady threw back her veil and hood,
and showed her pretty, radiant face to the king
and all his knights. The knights murmured in
admiration, for she was very beautiful. But the
king cried out with joy, for he knew her now, as
he had not known her when the Black Knight
carried her away.

"You are sweet Nimue!" he exclaimed. "You
are she who showed me the barge in which I
rowed to take my sword Excalibur from the hand
that held it above the water! You are one of
those wonderful beings who love the world of
knighthood—one of the Ladies of the Lake!"

Nimue smiled, and let her veil fall again,
before she answered:

"Yes, I am Nimue, a Lady of the Lake!" said
she. "And you have fulfilled your promise to
me, King Arthur! From today I shall never be
far away from you. With the other ladies, my

fairy friends, I will come and go between the Enchanted Forest and the royal and knightly court of Camelot."

The
Hidden Fountain

"So I journeyed on, until I reached the summit of the steep, and there I found everything as the black man had described it to me. And I went up to the tree, and beneath it I saw the fountain, and by its side the marble slab, and the silver bowl fastened by the chain. Then I took the bowl, and cast a bowlful of water upon the slab; and thereupon, behold, the thunder came, much more violent than the black man had led me to expect; and after the thunder came the shower; and of a truth I tell thee, Kai, that there is neither man nor beast that can endure that shower and live."

YOU remember that Sir Gawaine had been the first of the knights of the Round Table to leap upon his horse and follow the fairy hunt. Perhaps because he was the first to ride away into Fairyland, he had, at one time, the most marvelous adventure that befell any knight in those wonderful days of romance.

It all came about through another knight, Sir Kay, who told a story of a hidden fountain which, he said, was to be found beyond the waters of the sea, bubbling up among the mosses in the very heart of another enchanted forest called

Broceliande. There were strange tales related
of this fountain—of its magical waters, its ferny
secrets, the mysterious white marble slab upon
its brink, and the fairy birds that sang in the
blossoming thorn trees set round about it. Whoever could make his way to the fountain would
be sure of the finest adventure in all the world.

When Sir Gawaine heard about the fountain
and the promised adventure, he did not hesitate
a moment. He took ship to Brittany, and took
his horse and his armor with him. When he
landed, he mounted and rode away over the
moors and through the villages until he reached
Broceliande. The enchanted part began in a
valley, which was the loveliest valley in the
world. Every kind of wild flower grew there,
and a sparkling stream splashed and bubbled
amidst the sunlit stones. Sir Gawaine followed
the stream until he reached a castle which shone
like silver, while below it splashed a waterfall in
which its bright towers were reflected. At the
door of this castle stood two beautiful boys
dressed in yellow satin, with gold crowns on their
heads and gold shoes on their feet, gold daggers
in their belts and white ivory bows in their
hands. When the sound of Sir Gawaine's horse
traveled up to the castle windows a tall man,
also dressed in yellow satin, came out of the
door and advanced to meet the visitor, and Sir
Gawaine, springing from his horse, bowed very
low indeed, for he knew that the adventure had
begun.

The man in the shining robe led Sir Gawaine into the castle, where twenty-four maidens sat in a row, embroidering twenty-four beautiful cloths. Six of the maidens took Sir Gawaine's horse, six carried off his armor to clean it, and six took away his travel-stained clothes and brought him a robe, silk-lined, shining, and soft. The remaining six waited on him with silver bowls full of clear water, and fine damask towels of green and white. Then they spread a delicious feast for him, and the man in yellow satin asked him where he was going.

When Sir Gawaine replied that he was going to the magical fountain, in search of high adventure, the man in yellow satin seemed delighted to have met so brave a knight. He ordered Sir Gawaine's horse to be brought round, and showed him the path that would take him where he wished to go. Sir Gawaine rode off bravely in his bright, newly burnished armor, and presently came to a sheltered glade, with a mound in the center, where sat an enormous black man, with only one eye set right in the middle of his forehead, holding an iron club in his right hand.

Around this ugly, black giant were grouped a thousand wild animals—stags and boars, lions and tigers, serpents and dragons! Sir Gawaine was very much startled, but he spurred his horse on through the crowd of fierce, growling beasts, and, riding straight up to the one-eyed black giant with the club, asked him, with a great air

of boldness, the way to the fairy fountain where
a wandering knight could find the highest of all
high adventures.

The great, black giant scowled at him with
his one eye, but answered the question. If Sir
Gawaine would ride a little farther down the
valley he would see, presently, the tallest, green-
est tree he had ever seen in his life. Under this
tree bubbled the fountain, and, by the side of
the water, was a white marble slab. On the slab
was set a bowl of silver, fastened with a silver
chain. Any knight who was brave enough to
fill the silver bowl with water from the fountain,
and then to pour the water over the white marble slab, would soon find himself in the middle
of an adventure surprising and dangerous
enough to satisfy the most courageous man in
the world.

All this the giant growled out unwillingly,
and the animals round him growled to keep him
company. Sir Gawaine was not at all sorry to
leave them, and to ride forward among the
shady oaks and pines. Presently he saw the tall
and beautiful green tree of which the big, black
man had spoken—and there, at its foot, half hidden by feathery ferns and plumes of meadowsweet, were the white marble slab, the silver
bowl, and the glimmering water of the fairy
fountain.

Sir Gawaine dismounted and, without a moment's hesitation, took the silver bowl, filled it
with water, and poured the water over the white

marble. In an instant, almost before he could spring on his horse again, the sky grew as black as night, a clap of thunder shook the valley, and a hailstorm came beating and rattling about the tall, green tree. Every leaf of the tree was beaten off, and then the storm passed, and the sun came out again. And behold! Instead of putting out fresh leaves, the tall tree seemed to blossom into hundreds and hundreds of little birds, which set to singing more sweetly and exquisitely than the sweetest, most exquisite music Sir Gawaine had ever heard!

Then, as he sat on his horse, entranced, a loud, deep wailing traveled along the valley, and down through the sunlight galloped a knight, who was the blackest of all the black knights ever seen before. He and his horse were like jet; his armor was like ebony. He wore a black velvet mask and carried a black linen pennon upon his lance. Furiously he rushed upon Sir Gawaine, who spurred his horse forward to meet the oncoming charge, with a loud, defiant cry.

For many minutes they fought beside the fairy fountain, and then Sir Gawaine gave the Black Knight a mortal blow. But he did not fall at once—he only turned his horse's head and galloped away, with Sir Gawaine after him. In a short time the high walls of a palace showed through the trees. The Black Knight galloped across the drawbridge and through the lifted iron gate. But when Sir Gawaine would have

followed, the great gate slid down between the
high walls again and shut him out.

Sir Gawaine, disappointed, got down from
his horse and peeped through the bars. And, to
his surprise, he met the gaze of a charming
maiden with curly, golden hair who, as he was
peeping in, was, in the same way, peeping out!

"Who are you?" said she. "And what do you
want?"

"I want to come inside!" cried Sir Gawaine.
"This is, I know, my particular Palace of Ad-
venture! Let me in, I pray you, to finish what
I have begun!"

The maiden nodded her head quite kindly.

"I have been waiting here for you a long
time," said she. "I always knew you would
come! But I cannot let you in when you might
be seen. Take this ring. Put it on your finger,
and you will be invisible, and then I will lift up
the gate!"

So Sir Gawaine put on the ring and became
invisible, and the maiden lifted up the gate and
admitted him. He went inside, leaving his horse
to feed on the nice, fresh grass outside. The
maiden, who, he saw now, was dressed like a
page in pretty boyish clothes, bade him follow
her, keeping his hand upon her shoulder, for not
even she could see him while he wore the ring.
She led him to a wonderful gilded and painted
chamber where he took off the ring, while the
maiden kindled a fire, spread a silver table with
golden plates, and gave him a delicious supper.

When he had finished, she bade him listen to sounds of wailing that were coming up from below.

"The lord of the castle is dead!" said she. "He was the Black Knight of the Fountain, and has died from your blow. But it was always told that his lady should marry one of Arthur's knights. You must be he."

"Yes, I must be he!" cried Sir Gawaine. "This is my high adventure, I know. Fair maiden, let me see the lady!"

"Peep through that little grating, and you will see her in the hall below," said the maiden, preparing to clear away the golden plates.

So Sir Gawaine peeped, and, down in the hall, in a lovely black-and-silver gown, he saw a most beautiful lady sitting with candles all about her. She was pale and grave, but not very sad. She had never really loved the lord of the castle, but had, long ago, married him so that he might defend the fairy fountain, which belonged to her. Her name had always been the Lady of the Fountain, and she knew that she must marry again immediately so that those magical waters, that white slab with the silver bowl, that tall green tree, might still be kept unhurt in the secret fairy places of Broceliande.

She sat among her tall, lighted candles, her head on her hand. Sir Gawaine, watching her, felt his love for her spring up like a newly kindled flame. He turned to the pretty maiden in the page's dress.

"I love the Lady of the Fountain!" he cried.
"I have always loved her in my dreams! Take
me to her."

"Tomorrow!" said the maiden. "I will take
you tomorrow. Be assured she will love you in
return. I think that she, too, has always known
that you would come!"

So the next day the maiden gave Sir Gawaine
a beautiful robe to wear, with golden clasps in
the shapes of lions. He looked very royal in it
as he strode down the corridors of the castle into
the presence of the Lady of the Fountain, who
was sitting without any candles this morning,
thoughtful and all alone. The maiden led Sir
Gawaine to her, and she turned her beautiful,
pale face to him as he knelt silently on one knee
before her.

"You?" she said. "Then it was you who
fought with the Black Knight of the Fountain,
and killed him, so that he lies dead."

"It was my adventure, lady," said Sir Gawaine, softly. "He was only set to guard the
fountain while you waited for me!"

The Lady of the Fountain made a sign to the
pretty maiden who was dressed like a page.

"Call my nobles," said she. "I must speak
with them."

Then, when all the nobles came, she pointed
to Sir Gawaine, who was adoring her with his
eyes.

"He has shown himself the strongest knight
we have ever known," said she. "Tell me—for

it is for you to decide—shall he guard the waters of the fairy fountain for me, and for all of you?"

The nobles, who knew that Sir Gawaine had conquered in a fair fight, said that he should. And then the lady stood up on her raised throne, walked down the steps, and gave Sir Gawaine her hand.

"Be it so!" said she. "Be faithful in your charge, Sir Gawaine, and keep the fairy fountain and the tall green tree safe under the sun, the rain, and the stars forever!"

Sir Tristram's Tragedy

"Ah! would I were in those green fields of play,
Not pent on shipboard this delicious day!
Tristram, I pray thee, of thy courtesy,
Reach me my golden cup that stands by thee,
But pledge me in it first for courtesy."

SIR TRISTRAM was born in a country called Lyonnesse, and his mother was a great queen, who died when he was only a few hours old. After some years the king, his father, married again, and had more children—handsome little sons and pretty little daughters. But their mother, Tristram's stepmother, was very jealous of the prince, who was the child of her husband's first wife, and she tried to poison him. When the king found this out he was very angry, and ordered the wicked stepmother to be burned. But little Tristram burst into tears when he was told of this terrible punishment. He ran to the king, his father, and kneeling at his feet begged and prayed that his stepmother's life should be

100

spared. So the king pardoned her, although he could never love her again. But good, forgiving little Tristram was always kind to her, and after he had saved her life, the stepmother ceased being jealous of him and came to love him as if he were her own son.

He was brought up chiefly in Brittany, and then, when he had grown into a young man, he went to the court of King Mark of Cornwall. There everybody liked him and admired him heartily for his courage and his goodness of heart. He was musician as well as knight, and played the harp as beautifully as any minstrel, so that all the ladies of the court would sit together and whisper about him. They wished he would fall in love with one of them, but, although he was the very soul of courtesy and chivalry, he had no desire to marry any lady of the land.

After a time he went, as did all young knights in those days, to King Arthur's court, and in due time became a knight of the Round Table. He fought in many tournaments, and the ladies who watched would say to each other: "Here comes Sir Tristram. See the lions upon his shield!" For the lions were Sir Tristram's coat of arms, as they had been that of his father and his grandfather before him.

Then came a day in Sir Tristram's life which was very wonderful, and yet, in the end, very sad. He was sent to Ireland, by King Mark, to bring back a beautiful princess, called Iseult, who was to be King Mark's bride and take her

place as Queen of Cornwall. Sir Tristram set off
in a beautiful ship with silken sails and cabins
fitted up in silver and gold. He took his harp
with him, and also his shield, spear, helmet, and
sword. He did not know whether there might
not be many adventures waiting for him in Ireland, and he wanted to be ready for anything
that should happen.

Sure enough, no sooner did he reach Ireland
than he found the king, Princess Iseult's father,
in great need of help from the attacks of many
enemies. So Sir Tristram put his sword and
spear at the king's service and helped him in
many a fight, until the Princess Iseult began to
think that the young knight who had come to
take her to Cornwall was the finest knight she
had ever met. She used to take his shield and
rub it bright for him, and admire the three lions,
and say that Sir Tristram of Lyonnesse was indeed as brave as a lion himself. So that when
at last they set sail together for Cornwall, after
the King of Ireland had conquered his enemies,
the two young people were more than half in love
with each other.

But Princess Iseult would have married King
Mark, and probably have forgotten Tristram, if
it had not been for something that happened on
the voyage. You must know that Iseult had
taken her lady-in-waiting with her, and that the
Queen of Ireland had given this lady a magic
drink, in a crystal bottle with a gold stopper. It
was a love drink, a fairy wine, which would make

those who drank it together love each other for ever and ever, and care nothing for anybody else. This love drink, said the queen, was to be drunk by Iseult and King Mark on their wedding day.

Now it happened that the weather was hot and the sparkling sea seemed to make it hotter, and Sir Tristram sat on the deck of the fine ship in the sunshine and played his harp to beautiful Iseult. When he had finished his song and laid the harp down, she asked him to go into the cabin below and bring her something to drink, for she was very thirsty indeed from the warmth of the afternoon.

Sir Tristram went down, and there on the table he saw a pretty crystal bottle with a gold stopper, filled with what looked like sparkling wine. He carried it on deck to Princess Iseult, who took it eagerly into her hand, drew out the gold stopper, and tasted the fragrant drink. It gave her a delicious, cool feeling, and she passed the crystal bottle to Sir Tristram, and bade him also drink some. He did so—and then they looked at each other in amazement and rapture. They had drunk the fairy drink together, the drink which had been intended for Iseult and King Mark upon their wedding day.

Sir Tristram did not speak, but he took up his harp, and he played and sang the most beautiful and yet the saddest love song that was ever composed. Iseult sat with her lovely face hidden in her white hands, and her dark hair shining like polished ebony in the sunlight. The breeze rustled mournfully in the sails of the ship, and the waves had a sorrowful sound in them, as if the very mermaids and water nymphs were weeping for poor young Sir Tristram and sweet Princess Iseult. For never, never had two lovers felt love like that which had been hidden in the fairy drink, and which could not end in a happy marriage, because Iseult was the promised bride of King Mark.

So Tristram took his dear princess to Cornwall, and she was married with royal rejoicings, and her sorrowful knight went away and had many great and fine adventures for her sake. But they could never forget what they had felt when they drank the fairy drink, and remained faithful to each other until they died. And some people will tell you that they died on the same day, and that their bodies were laid side by side, and that out of their graves grew two fair climbing roses, which waved twined together in the sunshine, and dropped red and white petals to mingle softly upon the mossy ground.

The Foundling Prince

"Arthur is thy cousin. Go, therefore, unto Arthur, to cut thy hair, and ask of him a boon."

ONE of King Arthur's cousins was a little prince who had been found in a pigsty. The swineherd who found him, however, knew well enough that he was a prince, and took him up to the king's palace, where, after a little time, the king acknowledged him as heir to the kingdom. The prince's own mother was dead, but his stepmother, who was very fond of him, was determined that he should marry well. So when he was grown up she told him that only one princess in the world was worthy of him, and that was the Princess Olwen.

The Foundling Prince (everybody knew him by this name) immediately determined to marry the Princess Olwen, and set off to King Arthur's court to ask him for her hand as a kingly favor. For, in those days, anybody who wanted anything hurried off to ask King Arthur to give it to him. The prince rode on a fine black horse, with a saddle and bridle of crimson and gold. When he reached King Arthur's palace, the doorkeeper thought he had never seen so fine a man, and admitted him almost immediately. The Foundling Prince begged the king to give him the hand of the Princess Olwen, and the king said he would gladly have consented had he ever heard of her. As he had not, he sent out messengers who spent twelve months in looking for her, but were no wiser on the last day of the year than they had been on the first. In great disappointment the Foundling Prince called Arthur a promise breaker, and said he would go home, taking the king's honor with him.

But this could not be allowed. King Arthur was too great a king to permit even a Foundling Prince to go home disappointed and empty handed. He summoned the bravest and strongest of his knights and warriors, and bade them set off with the prince in search of the Princess Olwen. So this wonderful band of strong and brave men rode away into the country, and, after some weeks of traveling, saw a great castle in the distance. Just as they arrived within call of it, they came upon an immense flock of sheep in charge of a shepherd; so they rode up to him and asked him to whom the castle belonged. He answered that it belonged to the father of the Princess Olwen.

Then these warriors from Arthur's court said that they had come to take the Princess Olwen to the king. Whereupon the shepherd told them that other strong and brave men had gone into the castle on the same quest, but that none had come out alive. He told them, too, that he was the brother of the lord of the castle who had stolen all his possessions from him and made him shepherd of the castle sheep. Then the Foundling Prince gave him a ring which the shepherd took home and showed to his wife, who was very much pleased and excited, for the ring was a family treasure, and she knew by what her husband told her that her own sister's son was near at hand. As she was talking to the shepherd about the ring, all King Arthur's messengers rode up to the house with the Foundling Prince in the middle of them. The shepherd's wife greeted them, and showed great joy at meeting with her nephew. They all sat down to supper, and, directly afterward, the woman opened a big stone chest, and out of it stepped a curly-headed boy. He was, she explained, the only son left to her out of twenty-four. The cruel lord had killed the other twenty-three, and she was obliged to hide this one in the chest to keep him safe. This shows what a dreadful man the father of the Princess Olwen must have been.

Then the shepherd's wife told her visitors that sometimes the Princess Olwen came to the cottage to wash her beautiful auburn hair, and that, if a message were sent to her, she might come that very night. So a message was sent, and, sure enough, the princess came. Her hair was indeed beautiful, and her skin was as white as the petals of the wood anemones. She wore a white dress adorned with medallions of apple green, and her flowing sleeves were apple green also. And wherever her footsteps fell, four white clover heads grew.

The moment that the Foundling Prince saw her he recognized her and fell even more deeply in love with her real self than he had been with the image of her in his fancy. She, too, fell in love with him, but told him she was afraid he could never win her. His only chance, she said, was to ask her father for her hand, and to promise to perform every task which the cruel lord should command. Then she mounted her beautiful white pony and went back to the castle, accompanied for the first half of the way by the Foundling Prince. King Arthur's messengers who followed behind remarked what a handsome pair they made.

The lord of the castle was a terrible-looking man, almost hidden in his own wild, long hair. Three times he tried to drive Arthur's messengers away with poisoned arrows, but, each time, they caught the arrows, and flung them back at the lord. So at last—as he was very badly hurt by the arrows—he bade them declare their desire.

Then Arthur's warriors put the Foundling Prince in a chair opposite the great chair in which sat the cruel lord. And the two began to argue, one against the other.

"You must root up the whole of that hill yonder," said the father of Princess Olwen, "you must plow it and sow it in one day, and in one day the wheat must grow and ripen. Of that wheat only shall bread be baked for my daughter's wedding. All this must be done in one day."

"It will be quite easy for me to do this, though you may think it difficult," answered the Foundling Prince, remembering what Olwen had told him about promising to do all that he was asked, though he saw very little chance of keeping his word.

"This may be easy, but there are other things that you cannot do. Only two men in the world can till the land and rid it of its stones. Neither of these will come for you, and you will not be able to make them. Another man has in his possession the only oxen that can possibly draw a plow over such wild country. He will not give them up to you, and you will not be able to get them. When first I met Olwen's mother nine bushels of flax were sown, and from the seed not a blade came up. I require you to recover the flax and to sow it again in the wild land tilled by the men who will not come, and plowed by the oxen you cannot get. When the flax has grown it must make the linen for the headdress my daughter is to wear at her wedding."

"It will be perfectly easy for me to do all these things," cried the Foundling Prince valiantly, "although you do not think it is easy!"

"You may be able to sow the flax and to reap it in time for the linen headdress to be made which my daughter is to wear at her wedding," said the lord of the castle, "but there are other things you certainly cannot do. Yet I require that they be done. I want honey that is nine times sweeter than comb honey, to put into the marriage drink, and I must have the famous cup of which so many stories are told to hold this sweet draft of wine. Then I will eat out of no dish at the wedding supper, but only out of the basket of plenty, into which any man in the world may dip his hand and bring out the food he likes best. Also, you must bring me the fairy horn, and the fairy harp, and the fairy caldron of which all the world has heard tell. The fairy horn will pour out the wine, the fairy harp will play without a musician, and in the fairy caldron meat may be boiled without a fire. Then I must certainly wash my head and shave my beard for the ceremony, and I can shave only with the great boar's razor. Nor can I spread out my hair in order to wash it unless I have blood from the jet-black witch."

"All these things I can easily get for you," boasted the Foundling Prince, looking severely at the lord's extremely matted and untidy beard and hair.

"I shall want fresh milk, too, for some of my guests, and nobody has ever yet been able to carry fresh milk into the castle. It always turns sour. There are some magical bottles in which it can possibly be kept sweet, but it is impossible for you to find them."

"I will find the magical bottles and bring the milk," cried the Foundling Prince, loudly and firmly.

"Yes, but even if I wash my head, my hair is so thick and matted I can comb it only with the fairy comb, and cut off its ends with the fairy scissors that hang between the two ears of the great enchanted boar who also carries the razor."

"It will be perfectly easy for me to hunt the great enchanted boar and bring you the comb and scissors as well as the razor," shouted the Foundling Prince at the top of his voice.

"In order to do so you will want the fairy hound, and the fairy leash to hold him, and the fairy collar and chain, and the great huntsman whose name is Mabon who was stolen from his mother when he was three days old, and has been lost ever since. Whatever else you can do you certainly cannot find Mabon."

"It will be the easiest thing in the world for me to find Mabon. What else is there for me to do?" demanded the persistent lover of the Princess Olwen.

It appeared that there were various other things for him to do, one of which was to persuade King Arthur to join in the hunt after the enchanted boar with the razor (which was fastened to its tusk) and the comb and scissors between its ears. The lord of the castle was quite

sure that King Arthur would refuse to do any
such thing—but the Foundling Prince knew better. His last task of all was to bring Olwen's
father the sword of a terrible giant. This giant
could be slain only by his own sword, and would
certainly kill anyone who tried to steal it from
him. But the Foundling Prince was not daunted
even by the thought of the giant.

"My lord and kinsman, King Arthur, will obtain all these marvels for me!" he cried fear-
lessly. "I will have not only your daughter, O
great lord with the unkempt hair, but I will have
also your life!"

So saying, he departed from the castle, and
all King Arthur's warriors departed with him.

They journeyed for a whole day and, in the
evening, arrived at another castle, where a giant
who was as black as ebony, met them at the gate.
When they asked him whose castle it was, he
said that it belonged to the giant with the mighty
sword, and nobody who went into it ever came
out alive. In spite of that, Arthur's warriors
went on and knocked at the door. The porter
who sat inside called out to them that nobody
could be admitted unless he could do something
nobody else could do so well. Whereupon Sir
Kay, who was among the warriors, answered
that he was the finest polisher of swords in the
world.

The porter carried this news to the giant,
who replied that his sword very badly needed
polishing, and ordered that Sir Kay should be

admitted. So Sir Kay was let into the castle and
the sword was given into his hand; and, after
polishing it and making it very sharp, he slipped
behind the giant and cut off his head!

Then all the warriors rushed into the giant's
castle and took the gold and silver that were
hidden in it. With this treasure and with the
great sword they traveled back to Arthur's court
and told him the whole story. And when Arthur
heard of the other marvels that had yet to be
performed he asked which of them had better be
undertaken first. In answer, the warriors told
him that it would be best for him to find Mabon,
the lost huntsman, who was stolen from his
mother when he was three days old.

Now, of course, Mabon had been stolen by
the fairy people, and only the fairy people would
be able to tell of his hiding place. Very close to
the fairy people lived the birds in the trees and
the stags on the mountains and the salmon in
the rivers. So first of all the warriors went in
search of the talking blackbird.

They found the blackbird flying about a glen,
and, when they asked her where Mabon could
be found, she said she would show them the way
to a certain fairy stag, who might be able to help
them, as he was many years older than she. So
off they all set to find the fairy stag. When they
found him, they told him that they were messengers of Arthur, and that they were seeking
Mabon, who had been stolen from his mother
when he was three days old.

The stag answered that he did not know where Mabon was, but that there was an owl who was much older than he, and who might possibly be able to answer their question. As they were Arthur's messengers, he added, he would lead them to the owl. Once more they formed a procession, with the stag and the blackbird in front, and moved on over the hills till they found the fairy owl.

But the owl could not tell them where Mabon had been hidden. All he could do was to lead them to another bird, still older than himself—the great eagle of the crags. And the eagle it was who told them of the great and wonderful fairy salmon.

The eagle had once tried to kill the salmon, but they had become friends afterward, and so, when the mighty bird led Arthur's messengers to the mighty fish, the salmon answered that he knew where Mabon was, and he took two of the messengers upon his wide silver shoulders, and swam up the river with them to the stone walls of an old city. And there they heard somebody crying and lamenting in a dungeon—and it was Mabon, who had been stolen from his mother when he was only three days old.

Then the warriors went back to Arthur's court, and the king gathered together an army and came to the old stone city and attacked the dungeon. After he had captured it, he set Mabon free and took him home to his own castle. And then they all began to ask each other which

marvel would be best to seek next, now that
Mabon had been set free.

This time they thought they would seek out
a certain she-wolf who had two wolf cubs that
she took out hunting with her. The cubs were
really enchanted men, and it would help everybody if they were set free. So they found the
she-wolf, and Arthur set free the wolf cubs, who
would certainly, had they remained in wolf
shapes, have interfered in the chase after the
great boar with the razor fastened to his tusk
and the fairy comb and scissors hanging between
his two ears. On the way back from this adventure with the she-wolf one of Arthur's warriors saved a whole ant hill full of ants from
being burned by a great fire that was sweeping
over the country. And the ants were so grateful
that they burrowed into the earth and brought
out every seed of the nine bushels of flaxseed
that the Foundling Prince had promised to take
back to the father of Princess Olwen.

Everything seemed to be going well, and the
marvels were really being performed, one by
one. But the fairy hound and the fairy leash
and the fairy collar still had to be discovered.
As Sir Kay was talking all this over with Sir
Bedivere, they suddenly saw a great smoke from
a great fire, and they thought it might be the
fire of a robber. They hurried off in the direction of the fire, and there sure enough was the
greatest robber that Arthur had ever hunted,
roasting some boar's flesh on a spit. And Sir

Kay, pointing to the robber's beard, whispered
to Sir Bedivere that only the living hairs from
that beard could make the fairy leash that would
hold the fairy hound with which Mabon must
hunt the enchanted boar who carried the comb
and the scissors between his ears and the razor
on his tusk.

So the two warriors hid themselves until the
robber had eaten so much supper that he fell fast
asleep.   Then they stole up to him and actually
managed not only to dig a great pit under his
feet while he slept, but to tip him into it without
waking him up. When he was fast in the pit they
plucked out the hairs of his beard, and then
killed him outright; and, as he was a very wicked
robber indeed, the world was better for his death.

Carrying the leash which they had made of
the robber's beard, they returned to Arthur's
court.   "Now," said King Arthur, "what is to
be the next marvel?"   And they were all agreed
immediately that it was to be the capture of the
fairy hound.

They had to search through many countries,
but at last they found the fairy hound in the Enchanted Forest itself, and took it home to Arthur's castle.   And now they were all ready to
hunt the boar with the comb, and the scissors,
and the razor.   But this boar was such an enormous and terrible animal that Arthur said they
would not set out upon the hunt until they were
quite sure it really had the comb and scissors
hanging between its ears.   So he made one of

his knights take the form of a bird, and in this
form fly to the mountain where the enchanted
boar was hidden. The bird knight flew right
down on to the top of the boar's den, and, indeed,
there were the comb, and the scissors, and the
razor. But, when he tried to snatch them in his
bird claws, he only succeeded in getting hold of
one of the boar's bristles, which made the fierce
creature very angry indeed.

For a time now Arthur decided to leave the
boar alone, and to obtain the magic caldron.
Now the caldron was in the house of a great
king, who kept all his money in it, and entirely
refused to part with it at Arthur's request. So
Arthur made war on him and conquered him,
and carried away the caldron, money and all.
And by this time everybody was amazed at the
things that King Arthur would do, rather than
break his promise to the Foundling Prince who
wanted to marry the Princess Olwen.

And now the day had arrived for the great
hunting, but all the enchanted boars of the
country heard of it, and turned out, themselves,
to fight the warriors of Arthur's court. Chief
among these great boars was a huge beast with
bristles like silver wire, that made a shining trail
as he rushed through the trees. Arthur's warriors and Mabon and the fairy hound had terrible battles with the boars; but at last the great
beast with the comb and the scissors and the
razor was driven into the river, not far from the
very city where Mabon had been found by the

two knights who rode on the shoulders of the fairy salmon.

Then while the huge creature lashed the water Mabon himself sprang upon it and snatched the razor from its tusk and hid it under his shirt. But nobody could reach the comb and the scissors, until a very brave warrior followed Mabon into the water and managed to get hold of the scissors. However, before either man could secure the comb, the boar scrambled out of the water and galloped off, never stopping for at least a hundred miles. Then King Arthur himself set off after it, with a whole host of knights, and at last they overtook it, and, after a terrific fight, got possession of the comb, while the enchanted boar was driven into the ocean and never was seen again.

Then King Arthur and his warriors took a short rest, after which the king asked if there were still any more marvels to be performed. And his knights answered that the blood of the black witch had yet to be obtained. So the king set off in search of the black witch and found her hiding in a cave, and she nearly killed two of the warriors the moment they entered her hiding place. But King Arthur instantly took his sword and leaped into the cave and cut the ugly black witch in two. And one of his attendants took the fairy blood and put it into a fairy basin to take to the father of the Princess Olwen.

Now as Arthur's messengers had secured the witch's blood and the magical razor and the fairy

comb and scissors, they thought that the other
tasks might wait awhile, and they all went back
to the horrible lord's castle with their spoils.
They sprinkled his hair and beard with the
witch's blood, and then, in spite of his struggles,
cut both of them off and shaved him as clean as
an ivory ball. Then, as the loss of his hair and
beard made him quite helpless, they found it
easy to chop off his head with the giant's sword.
Whereupon they took possession of the castle,
and all the gold and silver and jewels that were
hidden in it.

As the father of the princess was dead, there
was really no need now to trouble about the other
marvels that he had declared were to be performed for her wedding day. The Foundling
Prince therefore married her without perform-
ing them, and he and his bride and Arthur's
knights and warriors made festival for at least
a week in the castle. And for hundreds of years
afterward all the old folk of the countryside
would tell of the marvels which were performed
at the command of good King Arthur, in order
that the Foundling Prince might marry the
Princess Olwen.

Nobody rejoiced more at the performance of
the marvels and the success of the Foundling
Prince than did the blackbird and the stag, the
owl, the eagle, and the salmon, all of whom had
helped Arthur's knights to discover the place
where Mabon was kept in prison. These fairy
animals, as you know, were very, very old—so

old that they could hardly remember the time when they were young, and they had lived among the mountains and valleys for hundreds of years. The blackbird judged of time by a smith's anvil, near which she always built her nest. No smith had worked at the anvil since she came there, but every evening she had sharpened her beak upon it, and, by the time Arthur's messengers came, the anvil had been worn down to the size of a nut. As for the stag, he had sheltered each night under an oak sapling and had watched it grow into a great oak with a hundred branches and then wither away and die. But the owl, who was much, much older, had come when the whole valley was a wooded glen, and had seen a race of men root up the trees and plant others; and their remote descendants, and again theirs, do the same, so that the wood in which the owl was now sheltered was the fourth wood. As for the eagle, he had sat for hundreds of years upon a crag, once so high that he could peck at the stars, and which was now but a yard above the ground; while the salmon had been speared with fifty spears, which he carried about in his silver back until the eagle pulled them out for him. Everybody in those days knew the stories of the owl and the blackbird, the stag, the eagle, and the salmon, for these fairy animals had relations who lived in the Enchanted Forest, and the stag was first cousin to the white stag of the fairy hunt. There is little doubt that Merlin had ridden upon his back of a moonlit night, followed by the beautiful hinds and fawns. As for the salmon, he was the most wonderful of all these old, old creatures, and the reason why he had so many spears in his back was because many hunters had sought for him in the rocky pools, and thrust their long spears into him to try to bring him to land. But he had always broken away, for he was the greatest fairy salmon living, and knew most of the secrets of the world. The fishes caught by the Rich Fisher were the children, and grandchildren, and great-grandchildren of this salmon, and King Arthur knew very well what a wonderful thing it was that such a mighty and mysterious fish should have given his help toward enabling the Foundling Prince to marry the Princess Olwen.

Geraint
and Enid

"For Arthur on the Whitsuntide before
Held court at old Cærleon upon Usk.
There on a day, he sitting high in hall,
Before him came a forester of Dean,
Wet from the woods, with notice of a hart
Taller than all his fellows, milky-white,
First seen that day; these things he told the King.
Then the good King gave order to let blow
His horns for hunting on the morrow morn,
And when the Queen petition'd for his leave
To see the hunt, allow'd it easily."

KING ARTHUR held his court not only at
beautiful Camelot, but also at a place
called Caerleon. The castle there had seven
doors, with a handsomely uniformed porter
seated at each one to open and shut it when the
knights and ladies passed. These porters were
very clever, as they had to bar the way to enemies as well as to make it free for friends. At
night they went to bed, all except one who
marched around the castle from door to door.
This one had cat's eyes, large and green and pale,

122

so that he could see in the darkness just as well as in the light.

Now one evening a handsome unknown youth dressed in yellow satin came running up to the porter with the cat's eyes and told him that there was a mysterious white stag in the wood over the river. The porter hurried to tell Arthur; for, ever since the fairy hunt of which you have read, the king had vowed there should never be a white stag near his castle that he would not follow. So as soon as the dawn broke next morning, the whole court set off a-hunting —horns blowing, hounds baying, horses prancing—in a great state of excitement. The white stag meant a fairy adventure for one of the knights; of that everybody was certain. They wondered which knight had been marked today to travel deep into the Enchanted Forest and to bring back a fresh secret from Fairyland.

Now Queen Guinevere was late that morning, and the hunt was almost out of sight when she came tripping down the stone stairs into the castle hall. She asked where Arthur had gone, and was told by her ladies that he had ridden off to hunt a great white stag in the ferny woods. Guinevere pouted for a minute; then she clapped her hands joyfully and declared that she would go a-hunting after the king! So she and her maidens dressed themselves very quickly and set off on horseback, their pretty veils waving and their faces as bright and mischievous as the faces of children.

As they rode through the trees they heard a great galloping behind them, and up came one of the very handsomest knights of the Round Table. He had long golden hair, and a long golden sword, and a blue-purple scarf around his shoulders, with a golden apple at each corner. His legs were bare, the better to grip the sides of his horse, which was very strong and tall and had a long black mane and a tail that was even blacker and longer.

"It is good young Geraint!" cried the ladies when they saw him. "O handsome and brave Geraint, are you coming with us and with the queen?"

Now, Geraint had really intended to gallop after Arthur as fast as he could, for he, too, was late this morning. But, when the ladies asked him if he were going to escort the queen, he could not possibly say he was not. So he bowed very low, drew in his prancing horse, and joined the pretty company of maidens, giving up all idea of the adventure for which he had been hoping he was the chosen knight of the day.

But no sooner had he drawn near the side of the queen than the adventure, which he thought he had given up, came riding through the wood toward him in the shape of an enormous knight with his face quite hidden under his helmet. On one side of this giant stranger rode a lady dressed in royally rich brocade, on the other pranced a hideous little dwarf. As they trotted abreast through the wood, Guinevere pulled up her horse and stared at them in amazement. Then the newcomers also drew rein, and, standing still at a little distance, seemed to talk among themselves.

The queen, frankly curious, shook her horse's bridle, and trotted off across the turf to speak to them. The dwarf was the nearest to her, and, pausing as she came up to him, she asked him the name of the big knight with the hidden face. But the dwarf, who was deformed and horrible even to look upon, answered by striking the queen with a long wand that he carried in his hand.

Then from Geraint such a shout as you never heard before rang through the wood. All the ladies, too, cried out in anger. Before anybody could do anything, however, off galloped the strange knight, still with the lady and the dwarf on either hand. And off after them tore young Geraint, calling at the top of his voice that he would avenge the queen!

Such a chase the three led him, through the dense wood and over the mountain and down into a valley where you could see the towers and roofs of a great city! Through the city gates they rode, with Geraint still hard on their heels. He saw that all the people stood still and saluted the knight and the lady as they galloped past; and he noticed, even in his haste, that the court-yards of the houses were full of men who were polishing shields and burnishing swords and washing armor and shoeing horses. Then the

knight and the dwarf and the lady galloped up
a hill to a great castle. Its gates were immediately opened with sounds of welcome. The three
rode in and the entrance was closed and barred
behind them.

As Geraint pulled up his horse, weary and
bitterly disappointed, he saw that he was close
to a ruined palace which could be approached
by way of an old marble bridge that spanned a
deep river. He crossed the bridge, and was met
on the other side by an old man who wore very
ragged clothing, but whose voice was gentle and
whose manner was gracious. This old man in-
vited the knight into the ruined palace, where he
was met by an old woman, also in rags, but sweet
and dignified. With her was her daughter,
whose face and hair were beautiful though her
dress was of poor and rough cloth. They,
too, greeted Geraint in soft voices, and offered
him what they could in the way of meat and
drink.

As he ate, the beautiful girl, who was named
Enid, looked after his horse, and he watched her
with deep admiration in his eyes. Then the poor
old couple told him that they were the real lord
and lady of the city, but that they had been
turned out of their home by the Knight of the
Sparrow Hawk. He was the knight whom Geraint had been following, and he lived now in the
castle, and every year he held a tournament in
the meadow just below it. In this meadow a
Sparrow Hawk, set up between two high three-

pronged spears, was always the prize of the day. Whoever won it was called "Knight of the Sparrow Hawk" for a whole year, with the right to live in the castle and to rule over the land. But as the knight himself always won by fair means or foul, there was not really much use in anybody else entering the tournament and doing battle for the prize.

Geraint listened, and his heart beat high with hope. "I will fight for the Sparrow Hawk tomorrow," he cried. "I will conquer the knight whose dwarf insulted Queen Guinevere, and I will force him to return your castle and your riches to you from whom he stole them."

The poor old couple looked at him, then at each other, and shook their heads.

"No knight can fight for the Sparrow Hawk unless the lady is with him whom he thinks the fairest lady in the world. Long ago this magic was made in the meadow. It is because the Knight of the Sparrow Hawk never stirs without his lady that he is always able to win the prize."

"His lady may be beautiful, but she is not half so beautiful as your daughter yonder!" cried Geraint eagerly. "Never have I seen a maiden as fair as she."

The words were no sooner out of his mouth than the old couple rose to their feet in great excitement.

"If you indeed believe that," said they, "if you do really and truly believe it, then take our daughter with you into the meadow tomorrow!

We will find some armor for you, and she will
make it possible for you to win, because of the
magic of which we have told you."

The next morning dawned beautiful and
clear, and a great number of people gathered
very early indeed in the meadow where the
Sparrow Hawk was set up between the two
three-pronged spears. When everybody had
arrived, a great blast of trumpets was blown at
the castle gates. The gates were then flung
open, and out rode the enormous knight with,
as usual, the dwarf upon his right hand and the
lady upon his left. He drew rein, and his heralds
cried out proclamation. Was there anyone present who would come forward and fight for the
Sparrow Hawk that was set up between the two
three-pronged spears?

Nobody stirred, and the great knight turned
to his lady and bade her go, take the Sparrow
Hawk upon her hand, and bring it to him. But
just as she was about to set off, a young knight
in old rusty armor, on a very tired, half-lame
horse, rode forward; and at his side a maiden in
rags walked quietly, with neither shoes nor
stockings upon her little white feet and only a
coarse hood upon her head.

"My lady is fair above all others!" shouted
young Geraint. "Come! I will fight you for the
Sparrow Hawk and call down the magic of the
meadow to help me! Victory will be mine, for
the sweet maiden, Enid, is the loveliest and
noblest lady in all the land."

Then the two knights rushed upon each other with a great clash of arms, while the lady in the royal brocade and the lady in rags looked on.

"They clash'd together, and thrice they brake their spears.
  Then each, dishorsed and drawing, lash'd at each
  So often and with such blows, that all the crowd
  Wonder'd, and now and then from distant walls
  There came a clapping as of phantom hands.
  So twice they fought, and twice they breathed, and still
  The dew of their great labor, and the blood
  Of their strong bodies, flowing, drained their force."

Everybody had burst out laughing at Geraint—at his lame horse and his rusty armor, and at the beggar maid he declared was the fairest lady in all the land. But soon their laughter changed to amazement and admiration, for with right good will the young stranger hacked and struck and dodged his enemy, until he proved himself by far the cleverer and stronger. And at last a great ringing shout went up from the whole multitude of watchers for they saw the great knight of the castle thrown to the ground, were he lay, stunned and motionless. Whereupon Geraint rode up to the Sparrow Hawk, took it upon his wrist, and, carrying it to a very old man and a very old woman who stood among the crowd, presented it to them with the grace of a prince making an offering to his lawful king and queen.

Then another shout went up from the people! They recognized in the poor beggars their rightful lady and their rightful lord. Leaving Geraint to look after the fallen knight, they es-

corted the old man and woman back into the
castle that had been stolen from them. There
Geraint presently followed with beautiful Enid,
and with the great defeated knight bound in
chains. As for the lady and the dwarf, they had
already fled. But all the people were shouting
with excitement and gladness; for indeed they
were delighted to see their true lord and lady
restored to their own home.

Then sweet Enid went upstairs to her own
dainty chamber, where she had lived as a little
girl, and dressed herself in soft silks and a gos-
samer veil and long chains of shining gems. She
came down looking like a princess, and Geraint
fell more deeply in love with her than ever, but
asked her to put on her old gown again, in
which, he said, he would take her to Arthur's
court, and there they would be married. Also,
he explained, he could not marry his fair lady
until the insult to Queen Guinevere had been
wiped out. The Knight of the Sparrow Hawk
must ride after them to Arthur's court and must,
in his own person, apologize fully and humbly
for the behavior of his dwarf!

So they set off: Geraint and his lady, and the
knight in chains behind.

When they reached Caerleon, Geraint led
both his bride and his prisoner into the presence
of the queen. The big knight apologized and the
gracious king forgave him. In doing so he made
the conditions that he should go into the waste
places of the realm to right wrongs and uphold

*They saw the great knight of the castle thrown to the ground, where
he lay stunned and motionless.*

the goodly order of the king. But Geraint married Enid, with everyone's full approval, and the queen herself gave the wedding dress, and the happy pair remained at the court of King Arthur for the rest of their lives.

> "And Enid tended on him there; and there
> Her constant motion round him, and the breath
> Of her sweet tendance hovering over him,
> Fill'd all the genial courses of his blood
> With deeper and with ever deeper love."

Lancelot of
the Lake

"... Lancelot, the bravest knight
Of all who since the world was, have borne lance,
Or swung their swords in wrong cause or in right."

AFTER the day when King Arthur and King Pellinore and Sir Gawaine had followed the elfin hunt into the heart of Fairyland, most wonderful adventures began to happen, not only to them but to all the other knights of the Round Table. You shall hear of these adventures one by one. To brave the mysterious dangers of the Enchanted Forest and the Castle Perilous and the Valley of No Return was the greatest sign of courage that anyone could show. So, of course, when King Arthur came back from the hunt of the white stag and told of the things that he had seen and heard, every one of his followers wanted to go into Fairyland and see these marvels for himself. One by one they went, and, on their return, they told the story of their ad-

ventures, which, indeed, were as thrilling as anyone could wish.

The fame of Arthur's fearless knights was
soon spread far and wide. Every brave and ro-
mantic youth wanted to come and make his vow
of fealty to the great king who was the head of
such a gallant company. And among these
youths was a prince called Lancelot, who had
spent all his childhood in Fairyland, in a way
that you will read about in the following story.

He was the son of a great king named Ban,
whose castle was built in a valley between two
mountain ranges. When Lancelot was only a
little baby, a neighboring king, called Claudas,
came riding one day over the eastern range with
an enormous army behind him. This great, glittering army set up its tents all around King
Ban's castle and prepared to besiege it. For a
long time King Ban and his soldiers held out
against King Claudas and the great army, but
at last they were obliged to surrender. Their
food and water were gone, and the soldiers could
not get past the tents of the enemy to bring back
to the castle the badly needed meat and bread
and wine.

So then King Ban sent a messenger to King
Claudas, asking permission for himself and the
queen and their little son to leave their home and
to go and place themselves under the protection
of the great King Arthur. Claudas consented,
but only on condition that the castle be handed
over to him immediately. So poor King Ban

handed over his castle and set off very, very sorrowfully on his great war horse, with the weeping queen in the saddle behind him. On a second
horse rode their one faithful servant, carrying
the baby prince, Lancelot.

They rode a little way down the valley, and
then King Ban said he could not bear to leave
his beautiful castle without one look at it from
the top of the nearest hill. So the queen took
the baby in her arms and sat down by the side of
a beautiful clear lake; while the king and the
faithful servant rode together to the top of the
mountain.

For a long time after the sound of their
horses' feet had passed away everything was
very quiet in the valley. Nothing was to be
heard but the sweet songs of the birds, the whisper of the wind in the tree tops, or the stealthy
rustle of waterfowl among the reeds. The queen,
who had dried her tears, played almost contentedly with the baby, consoled by its beauty and
its merriment. By and by, however, she became
anxious for she thought that the king had been
away a very long time. The baby was now asleep,
so she softly laid it down among the meadow
flowers, covered it with her cloak, and with fearful steps set off on foot up the rocky path that
led to the top of the hill.

She had not gone more than a hundred yards
or so when she heard a queer chuckling laugh
behind her—not unlike the cackle of a water hen
among the rushes, only much longer and more

She saw her little baby in the arms of a strange and beautiful lady.

like the chuckle of a mischievous imp. She turned around quickly to see whence the laughter came, and an alarming sight met her eyes.

She saw her little baby, the most precious thing she had, ten thousand times more precious than the castle, in the arms of a strange and beautiful lady. This lady's gown rippled about her like water in the moonlight; her long golden hair was wreathed with forget-me-nots and silver shells; her white arms shone like alabaster, and she wore a necklace and bracelets of the most lovely precious stones in the world.

She had taken the baby on to a big gray rock, that jutted out from the land toward the center of the lake. She was rocking it in her arms and laughing. At the moment the queen caught sight of her she began to sing.

The words seemed to be a fairy lullaby, but the poor queen did not pause to listen. With a loud cry she set off, running, to rescue her little baby. But the fairy saw her coming. She sprang up on the rock, joined her two pretty white feet together, and with the baby still in her arms dived like a silvery shining arrow straight into the green waters of the lake. A sound like a clap of thunder echoed all down the valley, and a sudden wind lashed the water into white foam. The lightning played among the trees, like the flames of a witch's fire, and long, loud peals of laughter mingled with the terrible storm. It lasted only for a minute, then went as suddenly as it had come. Everything was still again; the

lake glimmered green and calm. But the fairy
lady and the baby prince had disappeared, leaving not a single sign of their existence behind
them.

The poor distracted queen ran up and down
the banks of the lake, wringing her hands and
calling out her baby's name. As she wept and
called, the faithful servant came hurrying down
the side of the mountain. He, too, was sobbing.
He said that wicked King Claudas had set fire
to the castle, which was blazing away into ruins,
and that King Ban was lying at the top of the
hill, dead with grief.

Then the queen dried her eyes, and folded
her hands, and spoke calmly:

"My husband has gone. My baby has gone.
My home has gone," she said. "There is nothing
left for me to live for. I may as well die, too."

But even as she said this, the abbess of a
convent not far away came walking, wrapped in
her cloak, along the banks of the lake. She was
a good and sweet woman, and she knew all about
the fairy in the silver robes, with white hands
and golden hair, who lived under the water. She
heard the queen's sad words, and, coming up to
her, she spoke consolingly.

"Poor Queen!" said she—"for, indeed, I
know you are a queen—be comforted! You have
not lost so much as you think you have. Your
little baby is in hands far safer than those of
any human nurse! For your husband, the king,
be content. He is at peace. For yourself, there

is a home waiting in the convent there among the trees. Dry your tears and come with me."

The abbess spoke so gently, and yet so firmly, that somehow a strange feeling of consolation came over the poor queen. She went to the convent with this good woman and found it was a beautiful and restful place. The abbess comforted her by telling her over and over that the baby was, indeed, in the very best of hands. So by and by the queen, who was tired of wars and troubles, settled down in contentment—although she never forgot her lost baby—and stayed with the good abbess in the peaceful convent until she died.

But what had happened to the baby?

The beautiful fairy dived down, down, down, carrying little Lancelot in her arms. As she dived, her silver gown mingled with the silver ripples and the shells and forget-me-nots floated away from her golden hair. Then far below her appeared the roofs and towers of an enchanted city. And now the water turned into a cloudy mist, and her robes spread out into two glittering wings. She was no longer diving, but floating on the misty air. Softly, very softly, she floated downward, till the bright streets and flowery gardens and the marble walls of the enchanted city showed quite clearly beneath. Then she stretched out her little white feet and alighted on the very tips of her toes, all among the tall green grass and fairy buttercups and daisies. And from every side beautiful ladies came running up to her, exclaiming and shouting and clapping their hands. They were, every one of them, fairies of the lake, and they were so pleased to have among them a little human baby that they did not know what to do.

Tiny Lancelot had been sleeping all this time, and, because he was in the arms of a water fairy, had been able to breathe quite comfortably all the way down through the lake. Now he woke up, and smiled at the pretty ladies clustering around him. When he smiled they all cried out, with greater delight than ever, that his eyes were just like their own forget-me-nots. They kissed him and hugged him and took off his little prince's clothes, and dressed him up in silvery gossamers, just as they were dressed themselves. Then they took him into one of the enchanted houses and gave him a wonderful nursery all to himself, where he had fishes to play with him all day long. And he was so merry and healthy that they called him the "beautiful foundling," or sometimes "the happy child." But the fairy lady who had brought him there, and who was the queen of them all, never called him by either of these names. She had but one title for him, that she used always, and her voice was very gentle when she spoke it. This title was "Son of a King." Because, you see, she knew that he was of royal human blood, and that some day he must go back to the world from Fairyland and play his part as a prince among his fellow men.

And how Lancelot of the Lake went back to the world from the enchanted city under the water you shall hear in another story.

The Knighting
of Lancelot

"Sir Launcelot du Lake in all tournaments and jousts and deeds of arms, both for life and death, passed all other knights, and at no time was never overcome but if it were by treason or enchantment."

YOU read about the baby prince who was stolen by the water fairy. He was very happy in the enchanted city at the bottom of the lake, the pet of all the water fairies, but the very particular pet of the queen, who would dance him in her arms, calling him "Son of a King." Little Lancelot would crow with delight and pat her beautiful green dress. In time he grew into a tall and handsome youth. The queen knew that she could not keep him with her forever, and so she put him in charge of a woodman, who lived in the forest that grew all around the waters of the enchanted lake. Every morning the Lady of the Lake would take him up, up, up through the green waters and set him upon the flowery bank and call the woodman to come from his home and lead the boy into the forest to spend the day. But because the lake was a part of Fairyland, Lancelot never knew that the fine city where he lived was really beneath the water. He imagined that he just walked out of it into the forest through the mists of the morning, and returned to it at night through the moonlight and falling dew. But the lady whom he loved as his own mother always stood on the edge of the morning mist to wave him forward, and waited under the moonbeams, of an evening, to welcome him home.

In the forest the woodman taught him all the craft of a huntsman: the way to find the little brown hares, the wild foxes, the great, strong-tusked boars, and the beautiful antlered deer. Lancelot grew clever and strong in his happy woodland life. He could shoot an arrow straight and true, shoe and saddle a horse, and climb the crags as high as the eagle's nest. How wonderful life, lived as the forest people lived it, seemed to him! So firm his muscle grew, so bright his young eyes, so vigorous and alert his frame! All day he was on foot, or a-horse, upon the hills or among the trees. At night as he slept in his home in the enchanted city under the lake he dreamed of doing noble deeds when he was a man.

Then one day as he hunted with the forest people he heard them talking of a great king who was named Arthur, and who was the head of a gallant company of gentlemen who called themselves the Knights of the Round Table.

Wonderful stories were told of these knights—
of their courage, their beauty, and their pride.
All that night Lancelot lay awake thinking about
Arthur; and the next morning, as the sweet
water fairy led him to the misty horizon that lay
beyond the enchanted city, he told her of what
he had heard and said that nothing, nothing,
could ever make him happy unless he were
allowed to go to Arthur's court and become a
knight of the Round Table.

"Son of a King," said the water fairy, half
sadly, half triumphantly, "I have guessed that
this would be your destiny! I have known I
could not keep you always, because you are—
well, what you are! But can you be brave enough
to join Arthur's knighthood! Can you take and
keep the great vow? Can you, forever, be courteous, without baseness, kind to all, pitiful
to the sad, generous to the poor, stern to the
guilty—and choose death, at any time, before
dishonor?"

Lancelot cried out that indeed he could. He
said that to join in the vow was the only thing
that he wanted in the whole world. So then
this Lady of the Lake bent her head and consented. And from that moment the preparations for Lancelot's departure to Arthur's court
began.

And such preparations they were! The water
fairy had a suit of armor made for him, all of
silver and pearls. She gave him a sword, long
and shining, and a white satin mantle, trimmed

with ermine. Then she dressed herself, also, in
a robe of gleaming white satin, with ermine and
silver upon the sleeves and hem. She chose her
prettiest maidens, and her sprightliest pages;
and she brought her fairy horses out of their
fairy stalls. From the enchanted palace she took
long rolls of silk; and she had the silk made into
tents, for shelter on the way. Then, with songs
and music, the beautiful procession set off,
passed through the mists that lay on the borders
of their Fairyland, and rode through the forests
and sweet meadows of West-over-the-Sea, on its
way to the castle of Camelot.

Arthur was coming back from hunting when
he saw this sparkling company, which traveled
toward him through the twilight, looking as if
it were composed of sea foam and stars. Astonished, he drew in his horse and waited. Then,
though he did not recognize her, the Lady of the
Lake rode forward in advance of the rest, as
softly as a pale moth might flit across the dusky
grass. Behind the fairy rode young Lancelot,
all silvery white in his beautiful armor and royal
mantle; so that, indeed, he seemed no less fairylike than the delicate shimmering lady in front
of him.

The fairy paused as she reached Arthur's
side, and looked very earnestly at the astonished
king. Then she waved to Lancelot to draw near
also.

"Son of a King!" she said to Arthur. "I
have brought you a good knight and true. He

also is the son of a king. Admit him to your fellowship, I pray you, and make him a knight of the Round Table."

Arthur turned in his saddle and fixed his eyes gravely upon the youth in the white, shining armor, who rode up to the side of the lady.

"He is only a boy," said the king. "Is he ready to prove himself? Has he done battle yet in any just cause? Has he suffered for the sake of the weak, protected the innocent, or punished the guilty?"

"Not yet," answered the fairy gently. "But it is his most earnest wish to do so."

Arthur turned to Sir Gawaine, who sat on his horse by the king's side.

"Take the boy to your chamber," said Arthur. "Let him watch by his armor tonight in the chapel by the castle. Then tomorrow bring him to me."

He saluted the fairy, still not recognizing this beautiful and gracious lady who had brought her son to be a knight of the Round Table. He had no idea, at the moment, that she was a fairy at all, cousin to the very fairy who had stretched a white hand and arm out of the water to give him his sword, Excalibur, nor did he know that she would one day save his life. The lady bent from her white horse toward Lancelot, kissed him tenderly, and placed a ring from her own hand upon his finger.

"Take this ring," said she, smiling gravely, "wear it always in battle. If you are hard

Sir Gawaine set him to guard his armor in the chapel.

pressed by an enemy, turn it upon your finger. It will make you invisible. Turn it again, and your armor will change color—from silver to black, from black to green, from green again to silver. Good-by, dear Son of a King! Good-by!"

She kissed him again and rode back to the white and starry company who waited for her in the gathering night. Then they all rode silently away, and the sparkle of them died out among the trees. But Lancelot, in his silver armor, followed the king and Sir Gawaine and all the rest of the knights into the castle of Camelot.

Sir Gawaine took him to his chamber, gave him meat and wine, and set him to guard his armor in the chapel, as all those who desired knighthood had to do. The next day he took him to Arthur on his throne in the great hall. There, for the first time, Lancelot saw Guinevere, the Queen.

And, when he saw her, her beauty and sweetness filled him with a great feeling of devotion. All unknown to her, he stooped and picked up a little knot of flowers that she had dropped. That little knot of flowers he kept till the end of his life.

And now the tournament of the day was announced, and the king said that Lancelot might take his part in it. So the young prince from the enchanted lake of Fairyland mounted his horse and rode with the knights into the meadow, where, very soon, a great mock battle began.

How they wrestled and fought and clashed swords and galloped their horses! It was one of the finest tournaments ever seen, and very soon all who were watching began to speak of the wonderful courage and cleverness of a young strange knight clad in silver armor that shone like sea foam and stars. But even while they were speaking, he disappeared, and a black knight was seen in his place, looking like some strange figure carved in ebony. Then the black knight vanished in his turn and a knight in green appeared, like some magician of the forest, fallen straight from the emerald heart of an oak. In another moment this knight of the woodlands was gone, and there was the silver knight again, flashing across the meadow like a beautiful comet! And so on and so on and so on! For the black knight and the silver knight and the knight in emerald green were, all and each of them, none other than Lancelot of the Lake, who was galloping all over the meadow, continually turning his magic ring!

At last the mock battle was over, and there was a great call for the silver knight and the black knight and the knight in emerald green. But only the silver knight came forward—and in his hand he held the trophies of all three!

The people who had watched the tournament knew that some fairy had been helping the silver knight in some mysterious way. So they were full of respect for him and cried out that he must indeed be made a knight of the Round

Table, must drink the cup of fellowship, and join in the great vow. And the queen smiled, as she looked on while the king knighted him, and, in memory of the water fairy, named him Sir Lancelot of the Lake.

Sir Lancelot, as he knelt before Arthur, felt all the love of his brave young spirit go out to the king and to his sweet lady, Guinevere. He remembered the little knot of flowers that he wore close to his heart, and he vowed to himself that all the rest of his life should be spent in the service of the queen.

The Maid
Who Mocked

"Man am I grown, a man's work must I do."

O NE morning when there was to be a great feast, King Arthur, surrounded by his knights, sat in the banqueting hall waiting, as was his custom, for some adventure before breaking his fast. Ere long, one of his squires came running into the hall and said, "Now, my lord, you may eat, for even now a young maiden has arrived who has sore need of your aid." No sooner had he spoken than there entered

> "A damsel of high lineage, and a brow
> May-blossom, and a cheek of apple-bloom,
> Hawk-eyes; and lightly was her slender nose
> Tip-tilted like the petal of a flower."

"How can you sit there, Sir King," she cried, wringing her hands, "when there is yet so much evil being wrought in your kingdom?"

The king took her by the hand. "Be assured, maiden," he replied, "that neither I nor my valiant knights rest when there are wrongs to be righted or evil ones to be punished. What is your need, and your name?"

"My name is Lynette," said the maiden, "and I am nobly born. I have come to plead for a gallant knight—Sir Lancelot, I crave—to come with me to the rescue of my sister, the Lady Lyonors, who is held prisoner by four evil knights in the Castle Perilous. Three of these false knights, who dub themselves Morning Star, Noonday Sun, and Evening Star, guard the approaches to the castle; the fourth, known as Night, and sometimes as Death, holds my sister within the castle."

"Fair Lynette," replied Arthur, "you know well that the Order of the Round Table lives but to crush those who commit wrongs or otherwise disobey the law. There is no one of my brave knights who would not eagerly go to the rescue of your noble sister. Be of good heart; none come to Arthur's court in vain."

Now it happened that a year before there had come to Arthur's court a youth who had begged of the king three boons. When asked what these boons might be, he had replied, "I ask as the first that you, Sir King, will permit me to serve for one year in your kitchen, and for this grant me food and drink—no more. When the twelve months have sped I will crave the other two boons." He was so handsome and tall and bore himself so nobly that the king suspected him of being well born and at once granted his first request. The youth was placed in charge of Sir Kay, who at once displayed a great jealousy of him, calling him "Fairhands," because his hands were large and white and well formed, and losing no opportunity to scold and insult him. The youth, however, had in Sir Lancelot and Sir Gawaine two good friends who did him many a kind deed.

While the king was deciding which of his knights he would send with Lynette, Fairhands came to him and said, "I have come to thank you, Sir King, for the food and drink that you have bestowed upon me for the past twelve months, and, now that the year has passed, to crave the two remaining boons."

"What are these other boons?" said the king. "The first," replied Fairhands, "is that I may have the honor of going to the rescue of this maiden's sister, and the second, that I may be made a knight by the great Sir Lancelot." The king smiled. "You shall have your requests, fair youth," he replied, "for truly you have served me well!"

The truth of the matter was that Fairhands —whose real name was Sir Gareth—was the son of a great king who had at one time warred against Arthur and done him a great wrong. So when young Sir Gareth desired to go to King Arthur's court and become a knight of the Round Table, his mother would permit him to go

only on the condition that his real name should
not be known; that he should serve until he had
proved his worthiness in the king's kitchen; and
that he should receive no pay but his meat and
drink.

When the maiden heard what the king said
to Sir Gareth she was very angry. "I asked,"
she said, "for Sir Lancelot's aid, and you have
offered me a kitchen boy. Should such have the
honor of fighting for my sister?" So murmuring again "a kitchen boy!" she walked haughtily
out of the banqueting hall, mounted her waiting
horse, and rode quickly away through the great
gate of the castle.

At this moment a page entered and told Sir
Gareth that outside there awaited him a gaily
harnessed horse and shining armor. Sir Gareth,
all excitement, sped out of the hall, and there, in
the courtyard, he found indeed as noble a steed
and as glittering armor as any knight could desire. Swiftly, he donned the armor and returned
to the banqueting hall where he took his leave
of the king and Sir Gawaine, who wished him
Godspeed in his adventures. As he again left
the hall, the king told Sir Lancelot to follow the
young knight. Quickly upon his heels as he departed followed Sir Kay, jealous of the honors
that had been conferred upon the youth and
determined to humble him if possible. Once
outside, Sir Gareth sprang upon his prancing
horse and set out in pursuit of the departed
maiden. He looked every inch a knight as he

rode with grace his plunging charger, his armor
sparkling in the sunlight, but, when he had at
length overtaken Lynette and offered himself as
her faithful knight, she replied with great disdain, "Come not near me! You still smell of
kitchen grease! And, moreover, have a care of
him who follows you!"

Sir Gareth turned and saw Sir Kay, who rode
up and said in a commanding tone, "Don't you
know me, Fairhands?"

"Aye, indeed I know you," replied Sir Gareth,
"I know you well for a false knight, and so knowing, beware of me!"

At this reply from his one-time servant, Sir
Kay charged at him in a great fury and would
have unhorsed him with his spear, but Sir Gareth
deftly turned aside the spear with his sword, and
with a swift thrust wounded Sir Kay so sorely
that he fell helpless from his horse. At this, Sir
Gareth turned to Lynette and said, "Lead, and I
follow!" The maiden touched her horse and set
off at such great speed that Sir Gareth was put
to the utmost to overtake her. At length her
horse, exhausted by the wild race, was forced to
halt. Then, as Sir Gareth drew up beside her,
Lynette said bitterly, "Why do you so pester me,
kitchen boy? Do you think that because, by
some trick, you have bested your master I shall
love you any the better?"

"Maiden," said Sir Gareth gently, "ridicule
and abuse me as you will, but my king has
appointed me your knight, and I shall not

"Come not near me! You still smell of kitchen grease!"

quit you until I have rescued your sister, the
Lady Lyonors, or suffered death in so striv-
ing!"

This reply made Lynette angrier than before, and she again started her horse and rode
swiftly from him, plunging, in her blind rage,
into the depths of a dense forest, so that Sir
Gareth had to strive his utmost to keep her in
view. At length when Sir Gareth had finally
come up with her, she said, timorously, "Sir
Kitchen Boy, I have, I fear, missed the road that
is guarded by King Arthur's men. This wood I
know to be full of thieves. Truly, you may yet
have a chance to prove that you can really
fight!" So on until the dusk the two rode until,
from the crest of a long hill, they saw

> "Bowl-shaped, thro' tops of many thousand pines
> A gloomy-gladed hollow slowly sink
> To westward—in the deeps whereof a mere,
> Round as the red eye of an eagle-owl,
> Under the half-dead sunset glared."

Soon they heard loud shouts, and out from
the wood ran a servant crying that robbers had
attacked and bound his master, and that they
were about to cast him into the lake.

Sir Gareth turned to Lynette. "My duty,"
he said, "is to go to the aid of this knight, but I
am still more bound to protect you."

Lynette smiled contemptuously. "You had
better return to Arthur's kitchen! You would
be safer there!" she retorted.

At this, Sir Gareth spurred his horse and rode at breakneck speed into the wood. Here he found six powerful robbers dragging a knight, bound and with a large stone tied about his neck, toward the lake. Fiercely Sir Gareth attacked the robbers, and ere long had hurled three to the ground, senseless; the others at the sight fled in dismay. Then Sir Gareth quickly unbound the knight and untied the stone.

Then said the rescued one, "Sir Knight, you saved my life. What return can I make to you?"

"None," replied Sir Gareth; "I saved your life because my king would have me do such deeds. I ask but one favor in return—that you grant this maid a night's lodging."

"That will I gladly do," replied the knight, "for I truly believe you to be one of the knights of the Round Table."

At this, Lynette laughed aloud and mockingly said that her companion was indeed, in a manner, of the Round Table, being a dishwasher in the king's kitchen.

Soon they beheld before them a stately, battlemented castle, and when they entered found a great feast prepared. With gracious dignity, the knight seated Lynette and Sir Gareth at the table of honor, whereupon, with a great show of indignation, Lynette sprang to her feet and cried that she was being insulted, that Sir Gareth had forced his companionship upon her, and that she would not sit to eat beside a mere kitchen boy.

Their host was greatly puzzled by her words, but declaring that, kitchen boy or knight, Sir Gareth had saved his life, he placed Sir Gareth at a lower table and, leaving Lynette alone in her grandeur, seated himself beside his rescuer.

On the morrow Lynette and Sir Gareth thanked their host for his hospitality and took their leave. Again Sir Gareth told Lynette to lead and he would follow, at which she said that she would fly from him no more, but that if he valued his life he would return to Arthur's court, for near by there was one who would surely slay him. Her words had no effect on Sir Gareth, and as they rode along, she constantly mocking, he ever silent, they came presently to a great, forbidding forest through which coursed a tortuous, steep-banked river. Spanning the river was a single narrow bridge, and beyond on a grassy slope stood a gay, golden silk tent glinting in the brilliant sunlight. Above the tent a crimson flag fluttered in the summer breeze, and before it, unarmed, a knight paced proudly backward and forward. As Lynette and Sir Gareth approached, the knight eyed them haughtily.

"Maiden," he shouted, pointing to Sir Gareth, "is this the champion that you have brought from Arthur's court to compel us to let you pass?"

"No, oh, no, Sir Morning Star," replied Lynette, "the king so scorns your prowess that he has sent but a mere kitchen boy. Indeed, he is no knight!"

Then Sir Morning Star called commandingly, "Arm me!" and at his words from the tent ran three fair girls dressed in robes of red and gold, whose bare feet twinkled in the dewy grass. Swiftly these maidens decked Sir Morning Star in armor, blue as a midsummer sky, and brought to him a blue shield upon which was engraved a silvery morning star.

For a few moments Sir Gareth stood silently gazing at Sir Morning Star, all the while Lynette cruelly taunting him. "Why do you stand there staring and shaking with fear?" she mocked. "There is time for you to flee, before the knight has yet mounted his horse!"

"Maiden," replied Sir Gareth, "I would rather a hundred times fight than have you abuse me and call me that which I am not."

At this he turned his horse and sped headlong for the narrow bridge, toward which Sir Morning Star was racing from the other side. So terrific was the force with which they met that both were hurled from their horses and lay for a moment stunned. Quickly they rose and continued the battle on foot, fighting so fiercely with their swords that Sir Gareth's shield was sliced from edge to edge. An instant later, with a mighty stroke Sir Gareth drove his enemy to the ground.

Crying, "I yield!" Sir Morning Star begged Sir Gareth to spare his life.

"That I will do," replied Sir Gareth, "on the condition that this maiden pleads for you."

"Indeed will I ask no favor of you, kitchen boy," said Lynette haughtily.

"Then shall he die," declared Sir Gareth, striding toward Sir Morning Star.

"Do not dare, base kitchen knave, to kill one so far your superior," cried Lynette, horror-stricken.

"I am proud to obey your command, maiden," replied Sir Gareth, bowing to her. "Sir Knight, arise and go to Arthur's court and say that his kitchen boy has sent you. And forget not to beg his pardon for breaking his laws. Your shield I claim in place of that which you have destroyed." Then, turning to Lynette, he said, "Lead, and I follow!"

Presently as they rode along, Lynette said, half shyly, "It seemed to me, kitchen boy, that as I watched you fighting on yon bridge the odor of kitchen grease seemed to fade! But I warn you again that you had better turn back. For close by there is the brother of Sir Morning Star who will surely destroy you."

Sir Gareth laughed. "When I washed dishes in the king's kitchen," he said, "a fellow-servant owned a dog which, when told to guard his master's coat, never ceased to guard it. You are like that coat, and I am the dog sent by Arthur to guard you!"

In a few moments they came to a bend of the river, which was shallow but very swift. Across the shallows seated on a blood-red horse and clothed in armor so burnished that it was blind-

ing in the sunlight, they beheld Sir Morning
Star's brother, Noonday Sun. "Who are you that
dares to trespass on my property?" he shouted
to Sir Gareth.

"He is a mere kitchen boy," said Lynette,
"sent from Arthur's court, who, by good chance
has defeated your brother and is even now bearing his shield."

When he had heard her words, Sir Noonday
Sun, with a great shout, dashed into the torrent,
where Sir Gareth met him halfway. There was
small opportunity for skilful use of arms, but for
the space of an hour the two fought, swords ringing loudly against helmet and shield, until, for
an instant, Sir Gareth feared that he had met
his master. By a rare stroke of fortune, however, at this crisis Sir Noonday Sun's horse
missed his footing and stumbled, and together
knight and horse fell with a great splash into
the angry stream. Unwilling to see Noonday
Sun drown, Sir Gareth put forth his greatest
effort and, after a severe struggle with the
whirling currents, laid his enemy's bruised body
upon the river bank. "Go you to King Arthur,"
he said, "and say that his kitchen boy has sent
you!" Then again, to Lynette, he said, "Lead,
and I follow!"

With naught but a saucy turn of her lip,
Lynette pointed. There across another bridge
stood the third brother, Evening Star, clad only
in his naked skin, which shone like burnished
copper.

"Why does the madman stand there naked?"
said Sir Gareth.

"He is not naked," replied Lynette, "but is
clad in toughened skins, so that, even though
you cut his armor from him, these skins would
turn the edge of your sword."

At this point Evening Star shouted, "Oh,
brother star"—for he had seen his brother's
shield on Sir Gareth's arm—"have you well slain
the maiden's champion?"

"He is no brother of yours," cried Lynette,
"but a star from Arthur's court who has bested
your two brothers and will do the like to you!"

Then Evening Star blew a great blast on his
horn, and to him from a dingy weather-stained
tent came a withered hag bearing ancient rusty
armor and a shield on which was a half-tar-
nished, half-bright evening star. No sooner was
Sir Evening Star so armed and mounted on his
decrepit steed than Sir Gareth charged, and together the two met and fought with the greatest
ferocity until Sir Gareth hurled Evening Star to
the ground. Time and again this happened, but
always Evening Star was on his feet again in a
moment until, as his breath began to fail him,
Sir Gareth was overcome with a feeling of despair. But as his heart began to fail him, he
heard Lynette crying in a very different tone
from her former mocking one, "Well done,
kitchen-boy knight! O kitchen boy, brave as
any knight, strike and strike hard, for you are
indeed worthy of the Round Table!"

Thus aroused to greater efforts, Sir Gareth
hewed with his sword great pieces from Evening
Star's armor, but he could make no impression
on the hardened skin underneath. At length,
though, with one fearful stroke he severed the
other knight's sword at the hilt and felt that
victory was his. Then, against all rules of knighthood, Evening Star threw his great arms around
him and so crushed him, even through his armor,
that Sir Gareth could scarcely draw a breath.
With one final mighty, despairing effort Sir
Gareth gathered his remaining strength and
hurled Sir Evening Star over the side of the
bridge, and, staggering toward Lynette, left him
to sink or swim. When he had arrived, exhausted, at the maid's side, he said once more,
"Lead, and I follow!"

Lynette blushed a rosy red and with downcast eyes replied, "No longer shall I lead!
Henceforth, you, the kingliest of all kitchen
boys, shall ride by my side. Sir—and truly I am
inclined to add Knight—I am deeply ashamed
that I have so mocked and abused you. I ask
your pardon, for you have ever treated me with
courtesy, and, furthermore, you are as brave and
meek as any of great King Arthur's knights. I
am consumed with curiosity to know what name
you bear."

"Maiden," replied Sir Gareth, "you are not
entirely to blame, though you should have
trusted Arthur and should have known that he
would send with you none but one he believed

to be worthy. You have had your jibes; I have
replied with deeds. Truly your jibes fought for
me! And now that you have spoken such fair
words, there rides no knight—not even the great
Lancelot—who could best me! But, look! Who
is this who approaches?"

Sir Lancelot it was, who had paused to carry
the wounded Sir Kay back to the court and, so
delayed, had but now overtaken them. That he
might not be known, he had covered the blue
lions that decked his shield. When Sir Gareth
turned and Sir Lancelot saw the star gleaming
on his shield he cried, "Ah, felon knight, now
shall I avenge my friend!"

In reply, Sir Gareth put spurs to his steed,
but as he charged upon Sir Lancelot, the great
knight, with a dexterous thrust of his spear,
sent Sir Gareth sliding gently from his horse.
As he touched the ground, Sir Gareth laughed
aloud.

His laughter infuriated the watching Lynette. "How can you laugh?" she cried, "when
you have been so shamefully overthrown? Why
do you laugh? Because of your recent vain
boast?"

"I laugh, noble maiden," Gareth replied,
"that I, the son of a king, and but now victor of
the bridge and the shallows should lie here
thrown by an unknown knight!"

Then joyful at hearing his voice and finding
him still alive, Sir Lancelot dismounted and
grasped Sir Gareth's hand. "Is it indeed you,

Lancelot, who have overthrown me?" said Sir
Gareth. "Then need I not be ashamed!"

At this, going over to where Lynette still
stood pouting, Sir Lancelot told her the true
story of Sir Gareth, whereupon she clapped her
hands and cried, "I am truly merry to find that
my kitchen boy is a knight and of noble birth!
But I have sworn to the black felon who guards
my sister that I would bring you, Sir Lancelot,
to lay him low. Now, if you go, he will first fight
you, and my knight—my one-time kitchen boy—
will miss the full glory of the high and well-
deserved adventure!"

"It is possible," replied Sir Lancelot, "that
this felon may know my shield. Therefore let
Gareth change his for mine, and take my
charger."

"How like Lancelot," said Lynette, "courteous in this matter as in all!"

Eagerly Sir Gareth seized Sir Lancelot's
shield and mounted his charger, and silently
they crossed a broad, peaceful meadow. A shooting star coursed over the heavens. "See!" cried
Sir Gareth, "there falls the foe!" And then a
moment later as out of the silence came the shrill
hoot of an owl, " 'Tis the felon pleading for
mercy!"

Suddenly Lynette clung in terror to his
shield. "Return, I beg you," she cried, "this
shield to Lancelot. He it is must fight. I could
bite off the tongue that has so mocked and
abused you. You have done wonders, marvelous

deeds, but even you cannot perform miracles!"

"Be that as it may, maiden," said Sir Gareth, "I will defeat this last felon or die in the attempt!"

And so on they rode, while gradually the stars disappeared one by one as thunder clouds gathered overhead. Suddenly Lynette cried, "There!" Then all grew silent again, for before them lay the Castle Perilous. Near by they saw on a flat field a huge tent shaped like a mountain peak and all black as midnight except for a red border that ran around it. Beside the tent hung a long black horn which, before the others could stop him, Sir Gareth seized and blew with all his might. Immediately they heard loud tramping within the castle and lights began to flicker here and there. Then high above them, looking very beautiful among the trembling lights, stood the Lady Lyonors surrounded by her maids. As her glance fell upon Sir Gareth she waved her white hand. Again Sir Gareth seized the horn and blew lustily upon it. At the sound, from out the huge tent came a monster in night-black armor, mounted on a coal-black horse, and on the armor was the figure of a skeleton with a skull on the helmet in place of a plume. The monster halted before Sir Gareth, but said not a word.

At this moment Sir Lancelot's charger, upon which Sir Gareth was mounted, neighed; at which sound Night's black war horse bounded at full speed toward him. At the first shock Night was thrown heavily to the ground. Slowly he rose, lifting with difficulty his heavy sword. With a mighty stroke Sir Gareth split the skull atop his helmet and, with a mightier, split in twain the helmet.

Then there appeared, not the head of death, but the face of a handsome boy who cried, "Spare me! My three brothers made me do this, believing that none would dare to fight such a terrifying figure."

Now indeed was Lynette proud of her kitchen-boy knight!

> "Then sprang the happier day from underground;
>   And Lady Lyonors and her house, with dance
>   And revel and song, made merry over Death,
>   As being after all their foolish fears
>   And horrors only proven a blooming boy.
>   So large mirth lived, and Gareth won the quest."

The Witchery
of Nimue

"And Vivien ever sought to work the charm
Upon the great enchanter of the time,
As fancying that her glory would be great
According to his greatness whom she quench'd."

MERLIN was growing very old now, and his work at Arthur's court was nearly finished. He had made the Round Table for the knights who took the great Vow, and he had set the Seat Perilous at the king's right hand. No knight had as yet ventured to take his place in that mysterious seat. If ever one or another approached it, the fiery letters would suddenly shine out, in golden flame, "This is the Seat Perilous." And the murmur would once more pass from mouth to mouth of those who sat at the Round Table, "That is the Seat Perilous! No knight must sit in it today nor tomorrow nor for many years to come!"

The great magician no longer rode on his fairy stag over the hills at nighttime, nor took on the disguise of a bright-haired, laughing youth. His beard grew very long and white, and he would sit outside the great doors of Camelot, singing to himself and playing on a harp that he held in his long magician's fingers.

> "Then fell on Merlin a great melancholy;
> He walked with dreams and darkness."

And with him, very often, in those days, would sit the fairy Nimue, who was, as you know, one of the Ladies of the Lake.

She had changed her name to Vivien, for Nimue was too strange a title for any human lady to bear. Since King Pellinore had brought her back to Arthur's court, she had behaved as much like a flesh-and-blood princess as she could manage. But she was never anything, really, but one of the Ladies of the Lake—a mysterious, elfin thing with mermaid's eyes that were green and dark like the shadows you may see in mountain tarns. She knew much magic herself and, in the old days, had often peeped in at Merlin, as he sat in his house with the seventy windows and the sixty doors. It had been in obedience to the old wizard's orders that she had helped to make the wonderful and high adventure of the fairy hunt, which had carried off King Arthur into the Enchanted Forest so soon after his wedding day. And now it seemed to her the old magician was growing weary of the world, and she thought that he would be happier to go away and live forever in Fairyland.

Then fell on Merlin a great melancholy.

Often she would persuade him to sing to her and also to tell her stories of the magic that he had made in his life. Her eyes would grow dark and bright with excitement as she listened, and she would twist her silken hair around her white fingers and tap her little feet on the grass. Then she would ask him to walk with her in the woods and meadows, and she would make wreaths of wild roses and lilies and hang them on her pretty neck and arms, as they talked. Or she would lead him to the ferny brink of a deep pool and ask him if it were not like the fountain in Broceliande over which the tall green tree bent its branches and where the little birds sang so sweetly after rain. And, when night fell, she would persuade him to wander farther and farther into the forest and to talk to her of the fiery dragon that had once lain coiled up among the stars. More particularly, she would speak of the seven rays that shone over the West—for, said she, she thought those seven rays were seven fairies, of which she herself was one.

Then she would try to make him speak of the Silver Table and the Rich Fisher and the Shining Cup, and would ask him where he had hidden the little book in which it was all written down. But this Merlin would never tell her. It had nothing, so he said, to do with any lady, let alone a Lady of the Lake. For he knew well enough that she was only a fairy from Fairyland. Yet she fascinated him more and more! Because, you see, he kept telling her secret after secret, so that she

was spinning webs of his own magic about him
all the time.

One night they had been wandering in the
woods together as usual, and Merlin, cold and
weary, was walking slowly home alone. Vivien
still lingered by the side of a lake in which were
bright reflections of the stars. She loved the
cool water with its deep, still shadows better
than any human home. But Merlin still turned
wistfully back to Camelot after his long days
with the fairy in the forest. Tonight he was
thinking deeply of Arthur and all the other
knights of the Round Table. Above all, he was
wondering when that knight would come who
could with safety sit in the Seat Perilous, because Merlin knew that this knight, and he only,
would be the knight who would be able to go into
that far mysterious place where Joseph had hidden the Silver Table and the Holy Grail.

As he thought about these things, suddenly a
voice came through the trees, and he saw an old,
old man leaning upon his staff, who spoke his
name, "Merlin."

"Who are you?" said Merlin, startled.

"I am Blaise, the hermit who christened you
many, many years ago. Merlin, I have come to
warn you. Your own enchantments are being
woven around you! If you go on teaching your
Lady of the Lake more of your secrets, she will
cast a spell on you that even you will not be able
to break, and she will keep you in Fairyland forever."

Merlin sighed. He tried to see Blaise's face through the shadows, but it was very dark.

"Good Blaise," said he, "what am I but half a fairy, myself? I have done, I think, all that I was meant to do. I have set King Arthur on the throne of his father; I have made the Round Table; I have explained the letters written in the Seat Perilous. The Shining Cup is still hidden, but I do not think I am meant to wait at Arthur's court until it is found. I should be glad to go into some far country—say, to Broceliande— and to rest there in the green forests forever."

Blaise waited a minute or two; then spoke again. "It may be as you say," he answered. "Perhaps your work is really done. It has been a good work, Merlin. The wicked mountain demons have lost much of their power since the Round Table was made. They will lose it all when once the Shining Cup has been found again. And for the Ladies of the Lake—well, they are kindly and helpful to men. Did they not give the king his sword Excalibur? So go your way, Merlin! Rest, if you like, forever by the side of the woodland fountain under the branches of the tall green tree!"

The hermit's voice died away, and Blaise seemed to be swallowed up in the shadows of the wood. But, slipping through the trees, he saw the bright nymph Vivien coming to him again.

"Great wizard," she said, putting her little cool hand in his, "Come! Come away with me to Brittany! Come to Broceliande!"

Merlin laid his arm round her shoulders. "If I should go with you to Broceliande," he said, "I do not think I should ever come back again."

"Never mind, never mind!" whispered the fairy, patting the old man's hand, "Only come!"

She drew him across the dim, dewy meadows until they reached the seashore. There, under the stars, a little boat was rocking—one of the fairy boats that belonged to the Ladies of the Lake.

"Come!" whispered Vivien once more. And this time Merlin consented without another word.

So they sailed away to Brittany and to Broceliande where the green tree grew over the magical fountain that Gawaine, and only Gawaine, had found. But the Lady of the Lake knew every inch of the ferny path that led to it. As she drew Merlin toward it she gathered the magic fern seeds and tossed them playfully about him.

"It is the Eve of St. John," said she; "the fern seeds would make even a human being invisible! What will they do to you, do you think?"

But Merlin only smiled at her in the moonlight, without answering. And they went on, side by side.

Then before them they saw white thorn bushes glimmering pale, and above the bushes the tall green tree. They reached the fairy fountain and sat down beside it.

"See!" said Vivien. "Here are the white marble slab and the silver bowl fastened by the

silver chain! But no knight is guarding the
fairy well tonight!"

"Why should it be guarded?" asked Merlin,
laying his hand on the marble. "The fountain
is mine—has always been mine! The secrets of
its waters are mine. This white stone is mine.
See! My name is written there!"

Vivien looked, and to her amazement she
saw letters of gold appear just for a moment on
the marble slab:

I AM THE STONE OF MERLIN.

They shone there exactly like the letters on the
Seat Perilous, and then they faded away. The
fairy drew nearer to the wizard, and he laid one
hand on her hair, while with the other he fin-
gered the silver bowl.

"Are all the secrets of Fairyland yours,
Merlin?"

"Most of them, sweet Lady of the Lake. Most
of them! They are strange secrets, but the
greatest of all lies under that stone!"

"What is it? Tell me! What is it?"

"It is the secret of sleep," said Merlin dreamily, "of sleep that can make a man lie and dream
from day to day, from month to month, from
year to year. I could almost wish I were folded
in such a strange, sweet sleep."

"Tell me!" said the fairy again. "Tell me!"

She was eager to know, half from curiosity,
half from the desire for power. And so Merlin

told her, at last, the song and the dance that would draw from that mysterious stone its great secret of unending sleep.

Then the fairy stood up, and, while he watched her, still dreamily, she began to sing, very softly, and to weave a fairy ring all about the tired old wizard, and the white marble slab, and the magic pool. And as she sang and danced Merlin's weary eyes closed and his head drooped low on his chest, down which streamed his long white beard. Then a little silver mist like pearly air crept up from the fountain and out from beneath the fairy stone. And the magician's head bent lower and lower until at last he lay beside the mysterious fountain in Broceliande, fast asleep.

Vivien stopped singing and dancing and stood looking at him in the moonlight, her eyes more like green water than ever. The leaf shadows flickered over her and over the sleeping wizard, and the pearly mist grew thicker. At last the dew from it seemed to sprinkle the fairy's hair, and she laughed, for it reminded her of her own lovely lake. So gathering her gleaming robes around her, she slid away like a silver shadow, back to her own enchanted waters, leaving Merlin sleeping soundly and calmly in the fairy mist under the tall green tree.

The Vision of
Sir Bors

"And so came a white dove, and she bore a little censer in her mouth . . . and a maiden bore the Sangreal, and she said openly: 'Wit ye well, Sir Bors, that the child is Galahad, that shall sit in the siege perilous and achieve the Sangreal.'"

SIR BORS was a very large knight, tall and strong, as you might have guessed from the sound of his name. One day he was riding along a grassy road when he saw a building with high gray walls and towers like a castle, half hidden among great clumps of fine trees. A river ran around it, and across the river was arched a stone bridge.

Immediately Sir Bors felt a great desire to enter the castle. He turned his horse's head that way and, trotting over the bridge, drew near to the beautiful building. A knight rode out through the gates and tried to stop his way. But Sir Bors fought him and conquered him. Then, sparing the other's life, he rode proudly into the courtyard of the castle and was met by the king who owned it.

The king's name was Pelles, and he was always ready to welcome a brave and merciful knight. He greeted Sir Bors courteously and led him into the great hall. And no sooner was Sir Bors inside than he felt a strange awe and wonder creeping over him. It seemed to him that this castle was not like any other castle in the world.

It was full of strange lights and shadows, whisperings and rustlings, coolness and perfume. Little birds, sparkling like jewels, flew about the gold and purple glass of the windows. Their wings were almost transparent; their heads bore tiny crowns. And, most beautiful of all among them, was a white one, like a tiny dove, that flitted again and again through the shadowy hall carrying in her bill a little golden goblet hung on three chains.

"Truly," thought Sir Bors to himself, "I am in the very heart of Fairyland!" And, indeed, with so much unusual and mystic beauty about him, it was not strange that he believed himself to be in the land of the fairies.

Then, while the dove still flitted about the hall, a table mysteriously appeared, covered with honeyed cakes and ripe fruits and crystal goblets filled with crimson wine. The knight and the king sat down to eat and drink. When they had finished, Sir Bors felt so light in body, so refreshed, so calm and rested, that he wondered

what sort of fairy food he had been eating. As
he wondered he looked up and saw King Pelles
watching him.

"Sir Bors," said the king, gently and gravely,
"you have always been a good and pure knight."

"I hope so," answered Sir Bors. "I have
wished to be and striven to be all my life."

"You must have been," replied the king, "or
you would never have seen the little white dove,
nor have eaten the mysterious food on the mysterious table. And now something still more
wonderful is going to be shown to you."

As the king finished speaking, the hall grew
darker, and, at the far end, a golden light appeared. Then in the heart of the golden light,
which floated all around her like a sunset cloud,
appeared a slim and beautiful lady who, Sir Bors
thought, looked like a fair princess. But when
he looked again he saw she was not an ordinary
human being. She seemed a sort of delicate
spirit, and she moved like a spirit through the
dim shadows of the hall, her feet barely touching
the floor, her hair shining like sunlight, pale
wings folded upon her shoulders, and pale hands
clasped around what looked like a wondrously
beautiful silver cup. From the mouth of the cup
rose a still flame like the flame of a candle, and it
was as if this flame shed all the brightness which
surrounded the maiden's form.

She passed slowly by, and Sir Bors watched,
breathless. Then he turned wondering to King
Pelles.

"Who is she?" he asked under his breath. "What is the cup that she carries?"

The king answered in a voice that seemed to come from very far away.

"She is—who she is! And of the cup you have often heard."

"Is it," whispered Sir Bors, "can it be the cup of the spirit world—the silver chalice that we knights call the Holy Grail?"

"Yes," replied King Pelles. "It is the Holy Grail. Here in this castle it has been hidden for years. But look again!"

Then Sir Bors looked again, and down the hall, in the very track of the golden maiden, stepping through the lingering fading radiance she had shed, came a princess with a tiny sleeping babe in her arms. She stepped softly toward Sir Bors and held the babe toward him, for him to look at. He thought he had never seen a lady so lovely nor a child so like a flower.

"This is my daughter, the Princess Elaine," said the king, speaking more softly than ever. "And the little child is her son, Galahad. He was born in the Castle of the Hidden Grail. He it is who will sit in the Seat Perilous one day, on the right hand of King Arthur, the seat that has been empty so long. But when Galahad takes his seat there——"

"What?" asked Sir Bors, touching the child very gently with his big forefinger. "What?"

But King Pelles did not answer. He shook his head and fell silent again. The Princess

Elaine smiled at her little baby and then at Sir Bors.

"It will be a wonderful day," she said, under her breath, "the most wonderful day that the knights of the Round Table have ever seen."

"We have had many adventures," replied Sir Bors. "We have seen the fairy hunt and followed the great white stag! We have done homage to the Ladies of the Lake, and have slain giants and killed terrible beasts and taken over the guardianship of the fairy fountain under the green tree. We have wandered in the Enchanted Forest and seen the fairy salmon and ridden on his back. What is this adventure that will come with Galahad—the little babe here who is to grow up into such a wonderful knight?"

But still neither the king nor the princess would answer. They only smiled and shook their heads, and told him to follow them up the stairs of the castle and they would show him a sight even more wonderful than all the rest.

So up the stairs of the castle went Sir Bors, with the king and the princess—who still carried the babe—leading the way. And as they went, the whisperings and the rustlings began again all around them, the little birds flew with them, while the staircase windows shed purple and silver lights upon their heads. Upon the princess' shoulder alighted the small white dove and bent low its head, murmuring and cooing, toward the babe and swinging the little golden bowl on the three slim chains toward the child's

fingers. And tiny Galahad awoke and caught at
the pretty shining thing and cried out with delight. Just ahead of the procession it seemed to
Sir Bors that the spirit of the strange castle, or
whoever that lovely lady might be, moved dimly
yet brightly, with the Silver Cup held in her
white fingers. And always the golden light that
came from the candle flame shone on her face
and hands and hair.

They went on—up and up and up. Then, just
under the high roof of the castle, they came to a
closed door studded with massive iron nails. The
maiden vanished, and Sir Bors thought she had
slipped through the door just as a moonbeam
might pass through the glass of a window. But
the king brought out a great gold key from his
pocket and put it into the lock. He turned it
with a grating sound and pushed the door wide
open.

Then, though all was dark on the staircase, a
great light, like the brilliance of a summer day,
poured out of the room under the castle roof.
The little birds flew in as if they had found their
home, and the white dove spread its wings, as
it perched on the princess' shoulder and followed
the rest. Then came a burst of song from the
joyful birds now settled among the blossoming
branches of trees; and the scent of flowers—to
Sir Bors it seemed like almond bloom—came out
of the room together with their music. But
when he peeped in expecting somehow to see a
garden, he saw—not a garden but a room full of

shadows. In the center of the room stood a table exactly like the Round Table in every way, except that instead of being made of oak it was made of the brightest, purest silver. And in the center of the table stood Joseph's lost Shining Cup!

Sir Bors stood and drank in the beautiful sight, with his soul gazing out of his eyes. Then because he could stand it no longer—for he seemed to be in the heart of some place that was far more beautiful than Fairyland—he hid his face in his hands. When he uncovered his eyes again, King Pelles had closed the door and Princess Elaine was singing the babe to sleep on the stairs.

"Go back to King Arthur," said the king. "Tell him what you have seen, and bid all the knights of the Round Table await the coming of Galahad."

King Arthur
in the
Castle Perilous

"And when King Arthur awoke he found himself in a dark prison, hearing about him many complaints of woful knights. What are ye that so complain? said King Arthur. We be here twenty knights, prisoners, said they, and some of us have lain here seven year, and some more and some less."

AFTER King Arthur and King Pellinore and Sir Gawaine had followed the mysterious hunt into the Enchanted Forest, they never knew at what hour of the day—or of the night, either—they might not hear the horns of Fairyland blowing, and catch a glimpse of the long string of black hounds streaming through the meadow grasses after the beautiful white stag with the silver hoofs and the horns that were like the branches of trees. Many and wonderful were the adventures that befell them— and not only them but all the other knights of the Round Table. Sometimes the fairy hunt led them into startling danger, sometimes into strange and beautiful places; but always they

found that there was a lady in distress to be rescued, a giant to be killed, a brave gentleman to
be helped, or something else to be done that was
included in the great vow.

One day Arthur was hunting with his
knights on the borders of the Enchanted Forest,
following a big stag, which was not, however, the
one with the fairy hoofs that shone so brightly
upon the moss. The king rode his horse far from
his companions, and presently overtook the fine
stag and shot it with a swift arrow from his bow.
The stag fell by the side of a river, and Arthur
dismounted to see if it were quite dead. As he
stood there, the dim thrilling notes of the elfin
horns came to him, and in an instant, on the opposite side of the water, he caught a glimpse of
the flying white deer of Fairyland and of the
shadowy speeding bodies of the coal-black
hounds.

Arthur's horse began to tremble. In another
moment it had broken free, and was galloping
home as fast as it could. It might well be frightened, for, as the fairy hunt disappeared into the
shadows, the entire forest grew as dark as midnight, while down the glimmering black waters
of the river a little ship came sailing, with a hundred torches burning in a hundred silver holders
and lighting it from end to end. Nobody was
steering or guiding the ship, but it sailed on as
if a clever hand were at the helm; and, when it
reached the place where Arthur stood, it swung
about on the water and lay rocking, as if it were

at anchor, close against the bank where the willows grew.

"Now here is my adventure!" said King Arthur to himself, quite joyful and fearless and filled with the thrill of high adventure. "It is plain that this little ship lit up with a hundred torches has come to take me somewhere."

In his green hunting dress he strode down through the willows and boarded the ship. Off it floated again the moment he was aboard. And when he looked up at the sails above his head, he saw that they were all made of white silk and embroidered with pink roses and poppies the color of blood.

The little ship went on down the river, and the flaming torches were mirrored in the dark stream like so many stars. The king seemed to be quite alone on board, when, all at once, rising up, as it seemed, from the water, twelve beautiful maidens appeared and made a ring about him, joining hands and dancing as gracefully as fairies dance on a moonlit night around anybody who is lucky enough to be able to see them. Then they all fell on their knees and said how glad they were that he had boarded the little ship, and what a delicious feast was spread for him if he would go below. So below King Arthur went and found a cabin hung with white satin. Silver candlesticks with clear-burning candles were set on a table spread with fruit and honey, white bread, and red wine. He sat down to eat, and the twelve beautiful maidens waited on him.

When he had finished, they led him to a room hung with crimson satin, and he lay down on a blue and silver bed and fell asleep.

But when he awoke the beautiful ship and the blue and silver bed and the crimson satin of the hangings had all disappeared! He found himself in a dark dungeon, lying on a stone floor with twenty other knights who were all groaning in the deepest trouble and asking one another if nobody would ever come to help them.

King Arthur sat up and rubbed his eyes. "Where am I?" he asked the knights, in astonishment, "and who are all of you?"

"Alas! Alas!" cried all the twenty together. "We are twenty prisoners, and we have been thrown into this dungeon by the cruel lord of the castle. And here he will keep us until we die of hunger, as many have died here before us. For we can only be rescued when a knight has been found who is brave enough and strong enough to fight with the lord of the castle and to conquer him. And that nobody is ever likely to do."

"But indeed there is now a knight among you who is quite brave enough and strong enough to try!" cried King Arthur. "Here is the adventure to which I have been brought by a little ship with silken sails and twelve dancing fairies aboard. Tell me how to get out of this dungeon, and I will soon challenge the lord of the castle to fight!"

Even as he said the words a light seemed to appear from nowhere, and he saw a beautiful girl dressed like a princess, standing beside him with a gleaming silver lamp in her slender hand.

"Follow me!" said the maiden. "I am the princess of this castle, and I will do everything in my power to help to save these poor prisoners."

Immediately King Arthur sprang to his feet and followed her, eager to help set free the suffering prisoners.

She led him out of the dungeon, and each of the twenty knights rose to his feet and followed, as soon as the fair lady had unlocked and opened the door. She took them all to the hall of the castle and gave King Arthur armor to wear over his green hunting clothes. And she pointed to a war horse that stood, champing its bit, in the courtyard outside.

"Mount the horse!" said she. "Take your sword, your shield, and your spear! The lord of the castle is in the meadow on his great black steed, waiting for someone to do battle with him for his prisoners. Every morning he waits, trotting up and down. But no antagonists ever come. They know too well how very small is the chance they have against him!"

Arthur was already dressed in the bright armor, and had taken up his shield and spear. But when he looked at the sword he shook his head.

"I cannot fight with that sword!" he cried. "Alas! Alas! Where is my magic sword, Excalibur?"

Then the beautiful lady laughed, put her hand behind her, and brought forth what looked like Arthur's own sword, Excalibur! And the king with great joy took it into his hand and set off for the meadow, with all the twenty knights, pale and thin, and trembling between hope and fear, walking two-and-two behind him.

This was indeed a great adventure—much greater than King Arthur suspected. For the ship was a witch's ship, and the twelve dancing fairies were wicked fairies, and the lady who called herself the Princess of the Castle Perilous was the wickedest fairy of them all. Because you must know, Morgain-la-Fée, Arthur's sister, had made herself Queen of the Water Witches, and she wished her brother, the king, to be killed. So she had set all this magic afoot, and had also stolen Arthur's real sword, Excalibur, and given it to the knight who was waiting for the king in the meadow, prancing up and down over the daisies on his great, strong horse.

When he saw Arthur coming, he rode toward him with a great shout, waving the stolen Excalibur around and around his head. The king spurred his own horse forward, and the two met with a ringing crash of steel. Over and over again they struck at each other, but King Arthur felt with anguish that his own sword was not striking keen and true. Then, even in the thick of the battle, he found time to gaze at the beautiful jewels in the scabbard of the sword that his enemy used so cleverly and well. And instantly the king guessed that some terrible treachery was at work—that the other knight was fighting with the true Excalibur, and that the sword in his own hands was not even made of fighting steel.

As Arthur realized this, he wavered in his saddle and almost fell. The wicked lord who fought him swung Excalibur high to strike the last blow. But, at that very moment, the waters of the river which flowed round the meadow were suddenly and strangely disturbed. Out of the sparkling foam sprang a figure no less sparkling, and across the grass swept a beautiful lady, with dripping golden hair, and a long silver gown trailing yards behind her. It was the water fairy who had brought up Sir Lancelot. She had heard from the moor hens and little fishes of the plot made by Morgain-la-Fée, and was hurrying as fast as she could to the rescue.

She swept past the twenty pale knights and stood poised on her little white feet just above the grass, half resting on the meadow flowers and half hanging on her misty wings in the air. She waved her white hands and cried out magical words in a voice that was as clear and musical as the babbling of the brook. And the wicked lord on the big horse dropped Excalibur almost into Arthur's very hands! The king seized his own good sword again by its jeweled hilt, and,

with a shout of victory, stabbed his enemy
through the breast. The big knight fell heavily
to the ground and lay there, very, very sorely
hurt.

His servants came running from the castle
and carried him in. He got better in the end, but
nobody cared much about that. What everybody
did care about was that the twenty imprisoned
knights were set free and went joyfully home to
their twenty faithful wives! The Lady of the
Lake slid back into her shining, babbling river;
Arthur, carrying Excalibur, galloped off to
Camelot; and as for the twelve wicked fairies,
and the thirteenth who was the wickedest of all,
no doubt they went on dancing forever on the
little ship with the hundred torches and the embroidered silken sails.

They were only water fairies, you see, and
they had done what the Queen of the Water
Witches had ordered them to do. And, after all,
it had been a right noble and fine adventure for
King Arthur, and, as he had come out of it vic-
torious, he had no reason to complain.

Sir Perceval
and the
Silent Maid

"She prayed and fasted till the sun
Shone and the wind blew through her, and I thought
She might have risen and floated when I saw her."

SIR PERCEVAL was the seventh son of King
Pellinore, and, because he was the
youngest, his mother loved him best of all her
children. She would have liked to keep him a
child forever and was very glad that he was too
young to go to the wars with his father and his
six elder brothers. She wanted him always to
stay in the meadows near the castle, playing
with a golden battledore and a silver shuttlecock
among the flowers. But little Perceval was too
active and vigorous to do things like these. He
taught himself skill and strength by running in
the forest, by breaking sticks from the strong
trees, and by throwing them cleverly at targets
which he invented and set up all alone. And one
day while he was practicing with these sticks, he

saw three of the shining knights of the Round Table come riding through the wood.

In breathless excitement he watched them pass, and then ran full tilt to his mother in the castle and, describing these bright strangers, asked her who they could be. Now, the queen knew very well that they were knights, but she would not say so to her young son. She told him that they must be angels, hoping he would forget about them. But young Perceval squared his shoulders and felt the muscle of his arms. "If those are angels, then I will be an angel, too," said he. And he set off running after the knights as fast as he could.

He found them resting in a green glade, with their horses tethered to the trees, and they told him they were no angels but knights from Arthur's court. Then the boy examined their armor and the trappings of their horses and watched them wistfully when they saddled their steeds again and rode away. He was determined to join them, so he took a queer old piebald horse from a field hard by, pressed a pack into the form of a saddle, and twisted some supple twigs into the shape of a bit and bridle. Then, looking the funniest rider you ever saw, he trotted off on the piebald horse to his mother, told her that the shining visitors to the forest were not angels but knights, and that as he was now very nearly grown up, he meant to follow them to Arthur's court and be admitted to the fellowship of the Round Table.

His mother wept bitterly, but when she saw
he was quite determined she said that no king's
son could go to Arthur's court in that pickle; and
she gave him a suit of armor and a good horse
with as royal a saddle and bridle as he could
wish. Also she told him that if he wanted to
become a knight of the Round Table, he must be
courteous to all he met on the road and must
never fail to rescue any lady who called on him
for help. Then she kissed him good-by, and
watched him set off, quite alone, for he declared
that he would not have even a little page to keep
him company.

He rode for several days through the deep
forests and over the high granite hills. And
presently he saw the towers of Camelot in a valley by a river. So he rode down into the valley
and approached the castle gate.

Now at this time wonderful things were hap-
pening in Arthur's kingdom. Strange fires were
seen at night burning on the tops of the mountains, and sometimes flickering deep in the forest
glades. Voices and the music of harps were
heard when the moon was full; and the voices
sang of a great treasure which was hidden somewhere in West-over-the-Sea and which would
heal the whole world of ills if it could only be
found. In the evenings, when Arthur's knights
gathered about the Round Table, a radiance
would sometimes fall upon the Seat Perilous,
and the fiery letters that spelled its name would
shine forth again, as they had in Merlin's time.

And sometimes other writing glimmered there also—writing which said that the time was coming when the Seat Perilous would be filled. All these things made the people of the court wonder and talk in whispers together, asking what signs so strange could mean, and where the knight who was deemed worthy to sit in the Seat Perilous could be found.

Among the ladies of the court was a beautiful maiden who had been born quite dumb. Her lips were red and sweet and soft, but they had never formed a single word. Her throat was as white and round as the cup of a lily, yet it had never trembled with speech, nor swelled with pretty songs such as the other ladies sang. She sat all day over her embroidery, with quiet eyes and drooping head. But she seemed always to be listening—listening for somebody who did not come.

She was seated by the castle window when young Perceval rode through the gate. As her quick ears heard his horse's hoofs she raised her head swiftly. A great flush of joy swept over her pale sweet face, and she laid her embroidery down. Then she rose and, going into the hall, hid herself behind a curtain, rich with tapestry, which hung near the door.

Perceval was met in the courtyard by a knight who, when he heard the young rider's name, led him straight to Arthur and told the king that Pellinore's son had come to ask for knighthood at his hands. Arthur summoned

Perceval, but almost laughed to see him so
beardless and young. He knighted him, however, for his father's sake. But that evening
when the time came for the feast to be held at
the Round Table, the king bade Perceval go and
sit with the young unproved knights at the far
end of the hall. "For," said he, "you are not yet
old enough nor strong enough nor, I think, brave
enough, to sit with the tried knights at the
Round Table and to join in the great vow."

Then Perceval was very downcast, for he
thought he was going to lose his heart's desire.
He walked slowly and sadly down the great hall
and seated himself among the lesser, humbler
knights near the door. But at that moment he
heard a great murmur run through the banqueting room. Out from behind the tapestry came
the beautiful dumb girl, and as she walked toward him she spoke aloud.

"Rise from your humble seat, Perceval, the
noble knight and the chosen knight, and come
with me!"

She took him by the hand and he rose to his
feet and walked with her up the long hall, while
everybody watched in amazed silence. She led
him to the seat at the right of the Seat Perilous,
and pointed with her slender finger.

"Fair knight, take here your seat!" said she.
"For that seat belongs to you and to none other."

Then she went away as quickly as she had
come, and disappeared from the palace forever.
There were some who said she was dead, but

others said they thought she had gone away into the forest, for they had seen bright people come for her and lead her away into the shadows of the wooded hills. As for Sir Perceval, he stood by the seat which she had shown him, shy and hesitating. But King Arthur himself rose and, going to the young knight, took him gravely and kindly by the hand.

"Do not be afraid, Sir Perceval," he said. "We, the king and the knights of the Round Table, have watched the dumb maiden sitting day by day and hour by hour over her embroidery in the queen's chamber. We have seen her go to the window and gaze earnestly across the hills. We knew that she waited for somebody who would come. And now, as everyone has heard, her lips have opened at last. Who is there who shall not listen and believe when the dumb speak? Take your place next to the Seat Perilous! Be sure that no harm will come to you!"

Then Sir Perceval sat down next the Seat Perilous, and, as he did so, the far-off fires on the hills appeared again, and leaped into higher flames, and seemed to reach up to the very stars. The singing that people heard in the sky swept down to the roofs of Camelot and around the windows of the banqueting hall. The voices of the knights as they stood shoulder to shoulder and hand to hand, rang out in the words of the great vow and came to a sudden stop. It seemed to them as if something ought to be added to the vow today, but what it was they did not yet understand.

The time was coming, however, when everything was to be made plain, and when the whole world would know what it was that Merlin had written in the little book which he had hidden in his fairy palace in the enchanted wood.

Galahad

"My good blade carves the casques of men,
My tough lance thrusteth sure,
My strength is as the strength of ten,
Because my heart is pure."

* * * * * *

"All-arm'd I ride, whate'er betide,
Until I find the Holy Grail."

ALL the knights of the Round Table were at supper one evening when the adventure of Sir Galahad began. It began with a lady on a white horse, who rode in at the open doorway, calling for Sir Lancelot of the Lake. King Arthur pointed him out, and she beckoned to him with a queenly hand, and told him to follow her. So away they rode into the forest, the lady in front, and Sir Lancelot a little way behind.

She reminded him of his own fairy of long ago as she moved on, pale and beautiful, among the shadowy trees. Presently they came to a great building, and the lady dismounted and gave her horse to a page who hastened out to meet them. Sir Lancelot dismounted too; and the lady waved him good-by (he was almost sure, now, it was his own fairy) and disappeared into the building. Then, after a few moments, came a sound of singing, and a procession of women in white hoods swept out through the gates. In the middle of the procession walked a youth, slim, upright, and very fair.

"And who may you be?" asked Sir Lancelot, taking his hand.

The good women made answer for him. They all spoke together, and their voices rustled through the trees like a soft summer breeze.

"His name is Galahad!" said they. "His mother, the Princess Elaine, gave him long ago into our care. We have brought him up among everything that is fair and innocent. He is as beautiful as the young thorn tree that grew from Joseph's staff, and as pure as the snow that lies on its branches on Christmas Day. Take him to Arthur's court and ask Sir Bors if he remembers the baby in the Castle of the Hidden Grail!"

Then Sir Lancelot looked at Galahad, and the boy met his glance with quiet frank eyes. The good women said good-by to him and, sighing a little, went back into the castle, two-and-two together. And all through the night Sir Lancelot and Galahad rested under the forest trees. At dawn, Lancelot drew his sword and made the

A procession of women in white hoods swept out through the gates.

youth a knight under the shining of the morning star, saying,

"May you be good forever, Sir Galahad, for you are the most beautiful knight I have ever seen."

Sir Galahad lifted his face to the dawn and smiled. But when Sir Lancelot would have taken him straight to Camelot, he shook his head.

"Not yet," said he, gravely and mysteriously. "I will come at Whitsuntide."

So he went away through the brightening morning, and Sir Lancelot watched until he was out of sight. Then the older knight rode back to Arthur's court, reaching Camelot just as the evening shadows were falling and the knights were gathering together, as usual, about the Round Table.

Then before they all sat down, the same thing happened that had happened at the king's wedding banquet many, many years ago. Every seat began to glow with letters of shining gold, which spelled out the name of the knight who always sat there. And upon the Seat Perilous the letters flamed brightest and purest of all. But they read differently from the old mysterious warning, and the knights and barons reading, spoke to each other in grave whispers.

"The many, many years that Merlin told us were to pass before this seat might be filled have passed away."

King Arthur drew near and looked at the letters for a long, long time. He remembered

many things that Merlin had told him before the
great wizard fell asleep in Broceliande. At last
he turned to his own place at the Round Table.

"Cover the Seat Perilous with a silken covering," he commanded. "Let no one touch it nor
go too near. Something beautiful and strange
is about to happen to our great company."

Even as he spoke, a rider galloped up to the
door, and, springing from his horse, clanked in
among the knights, crying breathlessly, "Sirs!
Sirs! A great adventure is awaiting you all."
When they asked what it was, he answered that
on the waters of the river was floating a vast
stone that looked like red marble, and that from
it stood out a fair rich sword with a handle of
precious stones. And where was the knight for
whom the sword was intended if not among
those who sat at the Round Table at Camelot?

Then all the knights and the king and the
queen went down to the river, and, as they had
been told, there was the red stone floating with
the bright sword in the middle of it. Sir Lancelot, Sir Bors, Sir Geraint, Sir Gawaine, Sir
Gareth, all tried to draw it out, but in vain. Even
Sir Perceval failed. So they went back to the
darkening banqueting hall, where they seemed
to hear strange voices whispering about the
doors and windows. These, as the company entered, closed of themselves. As they closed, a
bright light, like a summer morning, filled the
hall, and a smell of hawthorn blossoms drifted
through it, with the song of merry birds. Then

Sir Tristram played his harp to beautiful Iseult.

before the knights had recovered from their
wonder, they saw standing among them an old
man with a long white beard, who had two
strange bright snakes twisting around his neck
and a harp in his hands. By his side stood Galahad, dressed all in crimson satin, with a mantle
of ermine hanging from his shoulders, and an
empty scabbard swinging at his side.

The old man stood close by the Seat Perilous,
and now he raised the silken covering with his
frail white hand. Then everybody saw that the
golden letters had changed a third time. "This
is the place of Sir Galahad, the High Prince," ran
the beautiful writing. And the old man took
Galahad's hand and drew him to the wonderful
seat.

As the young fair knight took his place, a
long murmur of admiration and gladness ran
around the table, and King Arthur cried out
aloud, "It is for Sir Galahad that the sword is
waiting—the sword which is fastened to the red
marble stone that floats upon the stream! Old
man, you have Merlin's look—Merlin's long
white beard—Merlin's wonderful wise eyes!
Tell us, is not this so?"

The old man bowed his head, struck his harp,
and began to sing. He sang the story of Joseph,
of the Rich Fisher, of the Silver Table, and of the
Shining Cup. He sang of all that the Round
Table meant, and of the new adventure to which
the knights must vow themselves from that day
—an adventure, not of lovely ladies nor cruel

giants nor strange fairy hunts, but a search, a
quest, for the treasure which had once been hidden in the strange gray castle where Sir Galahad
was born. This young, pure knight—so sang the
old man—was the first Knight of the Grail.
Now all the other knights of the Round Table
must follow in his steps. Only the pure, the true,
the good could ever find the lost treasure. Sir
Bors had had a glimpse of it—so, too, had Sir
Perceval, Sir Lancelot, and others. But to Sir
Galahad alone had it been a beautiful thing that
formed a part of his daily life.

While the old man sang, Sir Galahad sat
quietly in the Seat Perilous, his hand on his
empty scabbard. By and by he rose, and went
out of the banqueting hall, down to the river
which flowed black and silver through the night.
The stone rocked softly on the dark water, and
the handle of the sword glowed above. Sir
Galahad drew it from the red marble and went
back.

Then the knights all sprang to their feet and
acclaimed him, for they saw the fairy sword in
his hand. As they shouted their joy in him, the
hall went quite dark again, and everybody was,
as if at a signal, very quiet. For among the
shadows a flame like the flame of a candle could
be seen.

The slim flame grew and grew until it became a great soft, glowing light. In the red
heart of it moved a spirit who looked like the
dumb maiden. She floated through the hall, and

her feet made no sound. In her hands she held aloft the Shining Cup of the Grail.

The vision lasted but a moment before it faded. Then everything was dark again. But in the hush the old man began to sing once more, and the moon, suddenly shining through the window, showed Sir Galahad, clad in silver armor, the queer bright snakes that twisted about the old minstrel's neck, and the great company of shadowy knights seated at the Round Table, listening to the Song of the Holy Grail.

Pelleas and Ettarre

"We marvel much,
O damsel, wearing this unsunny face
To him who won thee glory!"

IT was the eve of a great three-day tournament which Arthur was to hold at Caerleon. Already the five hundred knights who were to strive for the golden circlet had begun to assemble. The ladies who were to view the spectacle were coming, too, each hoping that her favorite knight would win the prize and present it to her as the fairest. Through the dim woods and over the green fields they came with their retinues. Everywhere resounded the gay laughter of travelers, the pleasant clink of arms and harness, and scraps of song. All over the countryside blazed the brilliant color of rich trappings as these cavalcades wound over the crooked, stony roads. The very air was filled with merriment and tense with excitement and expectation.

214

The commons were gathering too, leathern-aproned smiths and armorers whose services would be needed in the coming days, vagabonds, ragged, whining beggars rattling wooden clack-bowls at the lords' and ladies' stirrups, sturdy, arrogant beggars demanding alms with a menacing scowl, swaggering woodsmen in Lincoln green, and not a few monks from the neighboring monasteries, their black robes tucked up in their girdles of knotted cord, their hoods thrown back, and their forgotten beads clattering at their sides as they strode along. All these little bands were in holiday spirit. They laughed, they joked, they sang, and the monks sang loudest of them all.

To all those who rode toward Caerleon the scene was a gay one. Even the knights of a hundred jousts felt their breath quicken as they looked upon it. Among the travelers was a young man who rode alone on his first journey from the barren and desolate islands which he had but newly inherited, and to him it was a scene from fairyland. All the knightly glory which the minstrels had sung at his father's court seemed here magnified a hundredfold. The high ideals of chivalry which his lonely youth had given him, the belief in the sanctity of knightly honor which his upbringing had taught him, were unspeakably intensified by the sight of these brilliant and stately companies which for some days had ridden by him. Now at last he had reached his goal for, coming through a thicket of beeches, he looked down upon a goodly valley with a silver river running through it, and, beside the river, a hill where rose the gray towers of the king's castle and the roofs of the town clustered about it.

Already the early comers had set up their gaily striped and colored tents beside the lists. Here and there a bright shield suspended from a bough or upon a spear displayed the device of the owner of the encampment and proclaimed him to be a knight of great attainments whose deeds had reached even the remote court of the lone young knight. Pelleas, Lord of the Isles, looked down upon the scene enraptured and, as the sound of the bells of a monastery, the gray walls of which showed through the distant trees, rose upon the evening air, he dreamed great dreams of the deeds he, too, should accomplish. Like many another youth, he told himself that his name would yet be sung by the harpers by the winter fireside as a very model of allegiance to the high vows of the Round Table.

However, his journey had been long and, now that it was so nearly accomplished, his excitement flagged. He sat down to rest a moment, presently stretched himself upon the ground, and soon was fast asleep.

As Pelleas slept he dreamed of the tournament. He won the sword and golden circlet. Then, when he was required to choose the lady upon whom to bestow the circlet, he remembered that he had no lady. He rode round and round

As Pelleas slept he dreamed of the tournament.

the lists, seeking among the spectators one fair enough to deserve the honor. However, when he found a lovely damsel and was about to place the crown of beauty upon her head, her countenance instantly became that of a hideous hag, and the derisive laughter of the spectators covered him with confusion. Slowly the lists faded from his sight. Slowly the blurred faces of the milling mob melted into a sea of forest branches tossed by the gentle breeze and gilded by the level rays of the late afternoon sun. He stretched lazily upon the purple heather, gazing with that delicious indolence of gentle awakening in which dream and reality are indistinguishably mingled, over the furze.

Suddenly a peal of laughter rang out close at his elbow, so like the laughter of the dream that Pelleas was not sure that he was yet awake. He looked up. There was a cavalcade of ladies and gentlemen and a large retinue watching him. Advanced a little from the rest was a tall knight in silver armor. He sat upon his horse, with one arm akimbo, and from beneath his raised visor gazed disdainfully upon the young man stretched upon the grass. Upon his saddle hung a small tilting shield, bright red, and adorned with three silver roses.

Pelleas scrambled hastily to his feet. Again the woods were filled with the laughter of the lords and ladies, and loudest and longest of all laughed the tall, arrogant knight in the silver armor.

"Ha, Sir Sleepyhead!" said the silver knight, "whence do you come, and what are you called that you sleep in the path of those who go to Arthur's tournament?"

"I am named Pelleas," stammered the youth, awkwardly enough, as he rubbed his eyes, "and in the country in which I was born I am called Lord of the Isles. My way also lies to Arthur's tournament."

"It is no place for sleepy boys," said the knight scornfully, "but perhaps the great Lord of the Isles can show the road to men who know the knightly art, and to these fair ladies who delight in valorous deeds. As his reward tomorrow he will learn, standing among the commons at the lists, how men of valor joust so that he can return to his own native Isles to practice safely with a broomstick at the quintain the arts he has observed."

"I go to joust, not to watch," replied Pelleas proudly, "as you may find tomorrow."

"What, boy!" exclaimed the knight, advancing menacingly toward him.

At this a lady, who seemed to be the leader of the party, rode quickly forward, and placed herself between the men.

"Back!" she commanded. "Is this the way to treat a stranger knight whose worship, for all you know, may be greater than your own?" Then, turning to Pelleas, she said with a winning smile, "Fair youth, of your courtesy direct our band of weary travelers to Caerleon."

So beautiful and so gracious was she, that all the anger which the knight's insolence had aroused in Pelleas vanished like mists before the morning sun. He led the party past the edge of the thicket and, with his eyes still on the lovely lady, pointed to the castle in the valley below. But long after they had gone, the beauty of the lady remained in Pelleas's thoughts. The more he thought of her, the greater her beauty seemed. He vowed that he would win the circlet and set it upon her forehead, and, if possible, that he would wipe out in the lists the insult of the discourteous knight of the three roses.

The cavalcade wound in and out among the trees down the winding road that led to Caerleon, and Pelleas followed it with his eyes until it was hidden by the foliage. When the sun, resting on the horizon, promised speedy darkness, he, too, rode down into the valley. Straight through the little city he rode and into the courtyard of the king's castle. There dismounting, he came into the presence of the king, and Arthur, who welcomed all strangers, received him right courteously. As this strong and handsome lad told his straightforward, manly story, and earnestly begged that he might receive knighthood from the king's own hands, the wise Arthur thought that never had he seen a youth more worthy of the high vows. He willingly granted Pelleas's request and, causing him to kneel before him, delivered the accolade, or sword blow on the shoulder. Then he put to him the high

vow of the order in the presence of all the Round
Table and of the many stranger knights who had
come to the tournament and were paying honor
to the king.

To some, the vow might be a mere formula
to be interpreted as each knight thought best,
but to Pelleas, filled with ideals, it was an oath
to be literally observed. As he withdrew from the
royal presence, he walked in an exalted ecstasy,
not of pride, but rather of duty. He accepted
knighthood, not as an honor, but as a sacred
pledge to do what he might in the cause of right
with unflinching courage and untiring ardor. To
keep his honor unstained, to protect the weak, to
be loyal and gentle and courteous: these were
the goals toward which he must henceforth
strive. All night he spent in solitary prayer in
the chapel. Clad in a long white robe, his armor
piled before the high altar, he prayed that he
might be worthy of the honor he had received
and strong to attain the ideals of his vow. If the
face of the fair lady whom he had seen that afternoon sometimes came between him and the
flickering candles of the altar, we must remember that he was but a boy, bred in a rude and
remote land where he had met but few women.
He could not be expected to see what others
would have said was a little cold, a little cruel, a
little worldly, in her face. Besides, she, too, was
an ideal, and an ideal is but a reality whose
meaner features are hidden by a gilding of enthusiasm.

A motley, milling crowd fills Caerleon. It is the first day of the great tournament. Noble and simple, priest and cutpurse, bowman and smith, merchant and mountebank throng the narrow streets of the little town and the fields surrounding the lists. The inns and wine shops are filled with revelers, peddlers hawk their wares among the crowd, little booths of green branches are set up here and there where refreshment may be had by the thirsty or the hungry. Song, laughter, noise, confusion are everywhere.

On the outskirts of the town are herded droves of cattle, sheep, and pigs which are to supply food for the throng attending the tournament. Some of the more tardy are yet coming along the roads amid clouds of dust, to the great inconvenience of travelers and to the greater inconvenience of their drivers when some haughty noble rides recklessly through the flock, followed by his laughing or swearing retainers.

Large crowds or little knots of spectators loiter about the hawkers and tumblers at the street corners as the entertainment they afford is more or less amusing. The vendors of relics of saints have disposed of enough pig and sheep bones to the superstitious to fill a respectable cemetery, and the hawkers of magical ointments, which will cure all ills, have taken from the trusting country folk more money than they have had in their pouches for many a twelvemonth.

About the lists little colonies of tents of all
the colors of the rainbow are set up, each with its
owner's shield near the door. The pages and armorers scurry about the camp on a thousand
errands with many collisions, much swearing,
more joking, and an occasional fight.

Now a late comer to the jousts rides into the
narrow streets, his brilliant retinue trailing behind him. After his supporters and men-at-
arms comes a lumbering baggage train. He
rides haughtily through the crowded street, paying no more attention to the commons who
crowd against the walls to let him pass than if
they were so many ants. Now and again his
purse bearer hurls a handful of small coins into
the mob, and a general scramble and many a
broken head is left in the wake of the cavalcade.
Men-at-arms pass with a devil-may-care swag-
ger, priests and monks shuffle along on wooden
sandals or ride past on sleepy donkeys. Presently a knight errant in worn and dented armor
jangles through the throng, and sends the crowd
flying to right and left to let him pass. He rides
alone or, perchance, with a solitary squire, but
the romance of his mode of life appeals to the
commons and they bear his boisterous reckless-
ness and haughty condescension with wide-eyed
respect.

Through such a motley crowd Pelleas forces
his way to the lists, alone, unknown, untried, and
only last night knighted by Arthur's grace. He
sits his horse in true knightly fashion, however,

and the bright eyes of many a fair lady follow
his well-knit figure as he rides along.

When Pelleas arrives at the lists, the spectators have already assembled. At one end of the
field are seats for the king, the ladies, and such
of the knights as are not to take part in the tournament. Outside the fence which surrounds the
field is the crowd, struggling to secure places
near the barrier, or retain the places already
won. Behind the crowd rise the tents of the
contestants, gay in their bright coloring and
fluttering plumes.

Presently there is a stir among the spectators. A silence falls on the babel of jest, banter,
and squabbling in which the commons are in-
dulging, as the heralds, with the royal arms upon
their tabards and embroidered richly upon the
hangings of their trumpets, advance into the
arena, blow a flourish, and formally announce
the opening of the tournament, the prizes, and
the contestants. The last being done with much
circumstance and repetition of titles of those
who are to compete, is hardly welcome to the
mob. They have come to see action. Long ere
the heralds have finished, their voices are lost
in a din of catcalls. But at last the catalog is
done, and another blast on the trumpets an-
nouncing the beginning of the jousts is greeted
with noisy approval by the commons.

Suddenly two gates at either end of the field
are thrown open and a band of knights rides into
each end of the inclosure. Truly it is a noble

scene. The armor of knights and horses shines in the sunlight; the plumes upon the helmets dance in the light breeze; painted shields gleaming ruddy and green and azure, or reflecting the colors of the precious metals, show an array of strange devices hardly to be conceived except in a dream. Armor clanks and jangles as the chargers paw and cavort in their eagerness for the fray. All is motion, color, and noise. The knights at each end of the lists lower their blunted tilting spears, and set the butts in their rests. There is a sharp signal from the heralds; with a wild scramble of horses, the two lines hurtle toward each other. Each knight chooses his opponent, and, as they meet, horses and men go down upon the sod. Shattered spears fly from mailed hands. Shivered shields drop useless to the ground. Those who remain horsed, dash on to the end of the lists opposite their starting place, wheel, and prepare for another onslaught. Squires rush to their masters with fresh spears to replace the broken ones, or to drag from the field those who have fallen and, because of the weight of their armor, are unable to rise. Again they charge. In lessened numbers the two lines close, and more go down. Again and again they repeat the maneuver until but two of the company are left, one from each side.

Their horses are jaded and the knights are plainly tired, but they take their places. Truly it is a meeting of heroes, for one has already un-

horsed nineteen of his opponents and the other
nearly as many. The arms of one are well known
—the hero of a hundred jousts—the shield of the
other bears no device. The mystery of the unknown knight whets the curiosity of the crowd
quite as much as his prowess. Some say it is the
great Lancelot riding disguised. As he passes,
ladies wave their scarfs and the commons howl
their approval. Even the king leans forward.
Beside the queen sits a fair lady whom she calls
Ettarre. It is she who since yesterday has en-
slaved Pelleas. As the unknown knight passes,
he turns toward her and raises the visor of his
helmet. It is Pelleas.

Pelleas and his adversary are again at the
ends of the lists. The jaded horses summon all
their strength. With a shout the knights are off.
There is no sound save the thud of galloping
hoofs. The spectators hold their breaths for this
final struggle. Nearer and nearer draw the
horses. More and more tense grow the watchers. A crash. They have met and both reel in
their saddles. The gay shield of Pelleas's rival
splits on the point of the young knight's lance.
Pelleas throws away his own shield, and the two
wheel to meet again. Pelleas drives his spear
against his opponent's helmet. The stricken
man rises in his saddle, clutches wildly at the
air. Off he goes over his charger's tail, and falls
with a resounding crash upon the ground. There
he lies stunned, while his horse gallops madly
down the field. The day's tournament is over.

Pelleas, the untried knight, has won the day. A hundred hands stretch up to help him from his horse; a host of ladies look admiringly upon him; the commons press forward over the barrier to catch a glimpse of the doer of such marvelous deeds. He rides slowly to the king, bows before him, and receives his praise. Then slowly he rides from the lists. Several young knights ride beside him, pressing him to take them in his train, and the rabble follows on foot, cheering their hero.

The second day in the lists found Pelleas a greater hero than ever, and when he had repeated his performance of the day before, there was little question among the spectators that he would win the sword and circlet. So it came about. And when the prize was bestowed, Pelleas rode to Ettarre and placed the circlet upon her head.

No doubt the lady was flattered, for she received the honor graciously, yet perhaps with a bit of condescension, as one who honors the giver in accepting his gift. However, for Pelleas his queen could do no wrong. He set down to his own unworthiness, and to his inexperience in the ways of courts, the somewhat flippant, half-contemptuous air which Ettarre showed toward himself. As for Ettarre, while it was very pleasant publicly to receive the homage of this brilliant young knight whose prowess had amazed the court and whose favor every lady was anxious to win, it was quite another matter to

endure the wooing of this awkward country
bumpkin, as she suspected him to be, which she
felt sure would follow any too cordial display of
gratification on her part. As has been remarked
before, those who knew Ettarre knew her to be
a cold and selfish woman. Now, indeed, she
showed these traits. She gladly accepted the
circlet and the plaudits of the throng which accompanied it, but their giver she treated coldly
and held at arm's length. The ardent youth was
hurt and disappointed by her coldness, but, filled
with the determination which had carried him
through the jousts, he resolved to win her respect at last, cost what the effort might.

And now the visitors began to disperse.
Long cavalcades of knights and ladies wound
over the hills, prolonging their holiday with song
and laughter as they rode homeward. Knots and
bands of the commons thronged the road, divert-
ing their journey with noisy jest and clownish
horseplay. But everywhere, among both gentle
and simple, the prowess of the young knight
Pelleas was the chief topic of conversation. So
modest and so courteous was he, withal, that he
had made himself beloved by everyone. By all?
No, one would gladly have thrust him from her
thoughts as she had repulsed him from her presence. Ettarre, whose smile he most desired,
hated him. Hated him without reason and
against all reason, as she was forced to acknowl-
edge to herself. And, since she hated him, in
her selfishness she would willingly have had him

killed to rid herself of his persistent court. She
spared him no slight, no humiliation. As she
rode homeward among her ladies and her
knights, free of him for the time, she plotted
how she might rid herself of him when he should
seek her out, as she was sure he would, and
what insults she might heap upon his devoted
head.

Meanwhile, Pelleas, too, was betaking himself from Caerleon. He, also, now headed a cavalcade, for several young knights had attached
themselves to him. Besides them were the harness and horses of the conquered knights. He
traveled with a heavy heart. So infatuated was
he by the beauty of the Lady Ettarre that her
face was continually before him, although her
cruelty smote him to the soul. And so these two
who should have left the tournament the happiest of all the throng were the saddest and the
most miserable.

At last Ettarre arrived at her castle and, in
the gaiety of her court, strove to forget her
persistent lover. Days passed and he did not
appear. Perhaps amid her satisfaction she felt
a bit piqued that he had not followed her as she
had expected he would. Perhaps in the more
solitary castle life, removed from the greater
splendor and the constantly changing faces of
Caerleon, she would have liked to see the ardent
young knight and amuse herself by teasing him
and humiliating him. At any rate, time hung
heavily on her hands, so one day, as relief from

the tedium of being shut up in the castle, she set out, accompanied by her courtiers, upon a ride through the forest. The party wound over the hills and among the great trees pleasantly enough for some time and, at length, came to a little clearing on the banks of a small, deep lake. Great was their surprise to see, as they approached it, a cluster of bright tents; and greater still was their surprise when from the camp rode out Pelleas. Clad in gleaming new armor and sitting his charger with courtly grace, he might well have won the approval of the most fastidious lady, but to Ettarre his presence was a challenge which she was quick to accept.

"How now, Sir Pelleas," she cried, "by what right do you trespass in our domain? The sight of you is hateful to me, as you know full well, and if you leave it not at once bitterly shall you rue your presumption."

"Lady," replied Pelleas, "I yet will win your love. Blinded by some witchery, you will not now listen to my suit, but I will break the spell by my devotion and my patient faithfulness."

"Think you, because by luck or, perchance, by aid of wizardry, you won the circlet at the tournament, you can in fair fight overcome my knights?" retorted Ettarre. "Begone, or I will harry you to the land's end."

While she was speaking, several of her knights had drawn into a rather wide circle about Pelleas, and, with hand on spear, watched narrowly their lady for any signal of action. It was a treacherous and unknightly manuever, but one which might be looked for from the followers of Ettarre. Ettarre worked herself into higher and higher rage. His patient courtesy through all her tirade incensed her beyond endurance. At last, trembling with wrath, she threw her hand toward Pelleas. "Seize him," she screamed.

With a bound, the waiting knights sprang forward. Surrounded on every side, the young knight's actions were as quick and telling as those of a cornered cat. He was helped by the rocky and tree-studded nature of the field, which interfered with concerted action by his antagonists, and by the fact that his horse was fresher than theirs which had been ridden many a weary mile. Pelleas with soldierly instinct was quick to take advantage of all these things. To his left, the ground was marshy, and the heavily laden horses would have difficulty in forcing their way through the long grass and thick underbrush; to his right, a steep, gravelly slope some eight or ten feet high, screened at its top by shrubbery, dropped sharply to the shore of the lake. Behind him, a small brook ran from the marsh down into the lake over a stony and precipitous bed; before him, the clearing extended for some distance, its floor at the further end being encumbered with fallen trees and rotted trunks, which gave an insecure and treacherous footing for the horses. Like the good soldier he was, Pelleas saw these things at a

glance. At the first signal of battle, the lover
became the fighter and his strategy was settled
upon. Wheeling sharply to the right, he
charged the two horsemen approaching from
that side. The stream behind him and the marsh
prevented quick action by his adversaries from
those directions, and the broken nature of the
ground prevented the knights in front of his
former position from changing the course of
their charge quickly enough to intercept him.
Pelleas was charging the knights on the lake
side from a position in front of and a little to the
left of them. While this left him in a good position to use his lance, his opponents were ham-
pered, since the spear was carried in the right
hand, by having their horses' necks between the
weapon and their adversary. The lances were
too heavy to be used effectively outside their
rests, and the horses were too heavily armored
to permit of quick maneuvering on such uneven
ground. Pelleas thundered upon them. Their
horses, stumbling over the vine-covered stones,
collided just as Pelleas's spear point met the
shield of the nearer knight. Horses and riders
were thrown backward into the underbrush, the
crumbling bank gave way, and steeds and riders
rolled down the bank to the shore. Their armor
was too heavy to let them climb the sandy bank
in time to assist their comrades, and, although
only bruised and shaken by the fall, they were
effectually removed from the remainder of the
battle.

Meantime, the knights who had at first faced
Pelleas had ridden past him, carried by the im-
petus of their charge almost to the brook, and
the knights in the marsh had scrambled to solid
ground. These last, Pelleas, circling to the left,
attacked upon their left flank. Here again he
had so maneuvered that he was safe from their
attack, while they must receive his lance in a
position which not only made counter attack impossible, but defence difficult. They gave way
and galloped in confusion after their companions, frightening their comrades' horses, and
packing all four knights upon the point of firm
ground which ran between the stream and the
sand bank by the lake. They were too closely
packed to permit the effective use of their arms,
and retreat was cut off by the steep and slippery
bed of the stream and by the precipitous gravel
bank. One determined charge by Pelleas and
they would be thrown into confusion, probably
some of them would have been cast over the em-
bankment or into the stream; then, while they
were still in disorder, he could have subdued
them with his sword. His antagonists realized
this, and tried to quiet their kicking, plunging
horses and place themselves in a position to resist the attack. Then a strange thing happened.
Pelleas reined in his horse, threw his good spear
upon the grass, and dropped his sword beside it.

"Seize him!" cried Ettarre, who had ridden
up. "Seize him! Bind him to his horse's tail and
bring him to the castle. Teach this presumptu-

ous boy for very shame to flee to his own barren isles and hide his face from the sight of men."

And so they rode homeward, jeering and insulting Pelleas, and he, although the way was hard and the insults pierced his soul, went willingly, for thus he might gain a sight of his lady.

One day a knight seeking adventures came into the country of Lady Ettarre. He was Gawaine, a nephew of King Arthur, and a knight of the Round Table. With him that morning was an old knight at whose castle he had lodged the night before, and who was courteously riding a little way with him as he departed. Presently they rode over the crest of the low hill, and there, spread before them, was a scene so lovely that they reined in their horses to admire it. A beautiful, rolling country it was with wide meadows and woods of ancient trees scattered over gently swelling hills that stretched away to the distant blue mountains. Here and there a bit of water sparkled in the morning sunlight, and above the far-off trees rose the towers and battlements of a large castle.

The scene was so happy and peaceful that Gawaine could hardly believe his eyes when a dejected knight, with his chin upon his breast, rode moaning and complaining from the forest into one of the meadows near at hand. But before Gawaine could ask his host the cause of this strange knight's behavior, ten knights rode from the forest on the opposite side of the

meadow, and, together, attacked the lone horse-
man. Gawaine, good knight that he was, prepared himself to go to the aid of the dolorous
knight, but so well did the unhappy man conduct
his defense, that before Gawaine could inter-
fere he had unhorsed all his antagonists. If
Gawaine was surprised at the sudden change of
bearing of the woeful knight he was certainly
unprepared for what followed, for after he had
defeated all his adversaries he laid down his
arms, and, without a struggle, permitted them
to drag him from his horse, tie him beneath the
horse's belly, and so carry him shamefully from
the field.

In amazement Gawaine turned to his guide.
"Why does so valorous and so strong a knight
permit himself to be so abused?" asked he. "In
spite of his sorrow, he seemed to me well able to
beat off his enemies, and to yield from choice
rather than necessity."

"The knight's name is Pelleas," said the old
man, "and never was there more valorous knight
or one better able to overcome his enemies, and
he does as you have just seen in order that he
may come to the Lady Ettarre, whom he loves.
For the knights you have seen are Ettarre's
knights, and ever she sends them against Pelleas
whom she hates, and they do right shamefully by
him that she may be rid of him, and ever Pelleas
returns and allows himself to be taken, as
you have seen, that he may have a sight of his
lady."

Then Gawaine bade farewell to his host and rode away. Before long he met Pelleas returning from Ettarre's castle, bitterly bemoaning his unhappy lot. Gawaine asked the cause of his woe and Pelleas unfolded the whole story of Ettarre's cruelty. He told how he had hit upon the scheme of allowing himself to be taken by her knights, for, each time, they took him to the castle, and there, even though the lady did nothing but revile him, such was his devotion that he accounted it worth all this unhappiness to see her fair face.

"Truly, it is a great shame that any lady should do such dishonor to so valiant and so true a knight," said Gawaine, "and gladly will I help you if I can. I am Gawaine, King Arthur's nephew, and a knight of the Round Table. Let us plan how I may win the lady's love for you."

Then they rode to Pelleas's camp and there planned and discussed and schemed and, at length, formed a plot to win the affection of Ettarre for Pelleas. And this was the plan: Gawaine should dress himself in Pelleas's armor, and go to Ettarre's castle. There he should declare that he had killed Pelleas, and, when she learned that so brave a knight was dead, she would, no doubt, be sorry for the way she had treated him and in her regret wish that he were alive again. Then would Gawaine tactfully expose the deception and plead Pelleas's cause. So certain were the young men that their scheme would succeed that both were eager to put it to

the test at once. Gawaine dressed in Pelleas's
armor and, mounting Pelleas's horse, promised
to return to him within three days, and set off
for Lady Ettarre's castle.

The four-mile road to Ettarre's castle lay
through a beautiful country, and to Gawaine, his
heart high with hope and adventure and his
spirit filled with youthful enthusiasm, it seemed
the fairest country he had ever seen. The path
skirted a small lake which reflected the dense
woodland and hills that surrounded it, and
whose surface was gay with floating white lilies;
the fragrance of the woods was in the air, and
not a sound disturbed the stillness save the call
of birds or the occasional splash of a fish leap-
ing from the water. When the road left the
lake's edge it wound through a deep forest,
around mossy trunks of ancient trees. Truly a
fairy forest, thought Gawaine, where any adventure might befall one. He half expected to see
a fairy or an elf appear from behind each rock
or tree trunk, but only an occasional rabbit scur-
ried across his path or an inquisitive bird called
to him from an overhanging branch. To be sure,
he did meet a bent old man gathering sticks, and
the old man said, "Gawaine, beware this quest.
Beware, lest bright eyes make you break your
faith," and, before Gawaine could answer, was
gone. This did cause him a bit of wonder. How
came the old man to be so far from any habita-
tion? What could be the meaning of the words
uttered in such a strangely prophetic tone? How

should the old man know his name, stranger as
he was and clad in Pelleas's armor? Could it be
Merlin, who often assumed such strange dis-
guises? For a little while he was puzzled and
uneasy, but the beauty of the landscape and the
lightheartedness of youth soon drove these
thoughts from his mind.

He rode on, singing at the top of his voice.
Suddenly, at an abrupt turn in the road, two
knights dashed toward him with leveled spears.
So sudden and so treacherous was the assault
that Gawaine hardly had time to lower his own
lance when they were upon him. He unseated
one, however, and avoided the other. Then he
wheeled his horse, and so vigorously attacked
the second knight that he quickly overcame him.
Both knights, on foot, now drew their swords
and ran toward Gawaine, but he, too, had drawn
his sword and gave back blow for blow. This
action seemed to surprise his attackers, who,
indeed, were two of Ettarre's knights on the
watch for Pelleas. They had expected an easy
bout, and were astonished at the change which
had come over the youth who had, before, let
himself be so easily taken. Of course they did
not recognize Gawaine in Pelleas's armor. Had
they done so they certainly would not have op-
posed him, for they had small stomach for hard
fighting. Gawaine reached down from his horse
and, seizing a knight by the visor, thrust his
sword close to his face. "Who are you?" cried
he. "Tell me or you die."

"We are Lady Ettarre's knights," said they, "and we but obey her commands. Full loath are we to harass so valorous and so courteous a knight, and gladly would we see you in Ettarre's favor. Now be advised of us and leave this quest, for know you well that never will she receive you."

Raising his visor, Gawaine replied, "I am not Sir Pelleas but Sir Gawaine, the king's nephew. Go tell your lady that I have slain Sir Pelleas and that no more will he trouble her with his love."

Then the knights went sorrowfully on their errand, for they had admired Sir Pelleas as had many another in Ettarre's train, and among themselves had condemned the conduct of their cruel lady.

Once more Gawaine took up his journey. Presently there arose above the trees the gray walls of a great castle. As he drew near, he observed much excitement on the walls of the castle, and when he approached the gate, knights and ladies came trooping over the drawbridge to meet him. Servants took his horse as he dismounted and conducted him to a great chamber, richly hung with tapestries, where sat Lady Ettarre.

"Never was guest more welcome," she exclaimed in greeting. "Truly you have done me great service in ridding me of the one I hated most of all men."

Ettarre's open joy at the news of Pelleas's death made Gawaine's undertaking more difficult than he had anticipated. The following days increased the difficulty, for Gawaine, bred though he had been in the plotting atmosphere of courts and used as he was to all the wiles and arts of courtiers, was not able to withstand the fascination of this clever and persuasive woman. Each day he struggled against disloyalty to his friend and unfaithfulness to his knightly vows. Each day he realized more and more that he was fighting a losing battle. Lavishly did Ettarre entertain him and she was constantly by his side. The days passed quickly in feasting and song and knightly exercise, and in the evening, while the minstrels sang old songs or composed new ones in honor of the guest, Gawaine and Ettarre watched the stars from some deep window recess, or, leaning over the battlements, listened to the old, wild, half-rollicking, half-sad songs of the men-at-arms gathered in little knots around the torches in the courtyard. No longer did Gawaine struggle against his love for Ettarre. No longer did he remember Pelleas or his promise to him. Forgotten were chivalry and the vows of knighthood. Only this was his desire: to remain always with Ettarre.

If the days sped quickly for Gawaine at Ettarre's castle, they dragged slowly enough for Pelleas in his woodland camp. Impatiently he waited the return of his friend, never for a moment doubting that so good a knight would speedily redeem his promise. Each hour brought disappointment and yet new hope. But

as the hours sped, the hope grew fainter. Never
did Pelleas doubt his friend's loyalty, but visions
of all sorts of accidents, of death at the hands of
Ettarre's knights, of imprisonment in the castle
assailed him. His squires tried to cheer and en-
courage him, but on the third evening when
Gawaine did not appear, Pelleas put on his
armor and, taking only his good sword, rode toward Ettarre's castle. As he rode, he carefully
examined the road for any sign of Gawaine and
tried to peer into the dark woods by the roadside,
half expecting to see there the body of his friend.
But the moonlight revealed nothing, and at last
the black outline of the castle rose against the
sky. Lights flared in the small windows, and
cressets upon the battlements sent a smoky
flame into the air. Music there was, too, that
even the thick walls could only muffle, but not
silence. Pelleas rode slowly toward the gate. The
drawbridge was down and the portcullis was up,
and Pelleas could see knots of men at arms singing and playing at dice by the light of torches
fastened to the wall of the gateway. Here and
there little groups of knights and ladies strolled
over the grass in the bright moonlight. Pelleas
dismounted and made his way toward the gate
in the shadow of the woods that surrounded the
clearing about the castle. Suddenly he heard
familiar voices. Withdrawn to some distance
from the rest and leaning against a great tree,
were a man and woman. Pelleas in the shadow
might have touched them.

In her hands she held aloft the **Shining Cup of the Grail.**

"Tell me again, beloved Gawaine, how you slew that most hateful of knights, Pelleas," said the woman.

"That will I gladly, dear lady," replied the knight.

Pelleas stood motionless. His friend faithless to him, faithless to knighthood! Ettarre gloating in his death! Pelleas reeled with the sudden disillusionment. If the king's own nephew so lightly regarded his vows, where was honor? If woman so fair could rejoice in the murder of one whose only fault had been adoring faithfulness, where should one find tenderness or goodness in woman? He drew his sword. He would confront them, and, when they had seen that he knew their treachery, he would kill them. He took one step. No! He could not kill a helpless woman and an unarmed knight. He slipped back, unseen, into the shadow. He sheathed his sword and stumbled back to his horse. Mounting as in a dream, with all the world seeming unreal, he turned his charger's head back toward the path by which he had come. The horse plodded slowly over the uneven ground and Pelleas bowed low over the steed's neck, not thinking or caring where he rode.

"Gawaine!" "Faithless!" "Ettarre!" "Heartless!" "Gawaine!" "Faithless!" "Ettarre!" "Heartless!" The slow plod of the horse's hoofs seemed to repeat again and again the monotonous words. Now and then a low moan escaped

Pelleas, but he was too dazed to think connectedly. Then the horse stumbled. As one awakened suddenly from a sound sleep, Pelleas wheeled his steed about. His brain worked quickly enough now. He had been betrayed. Death, only death, would blot out the crime against friendship and knighthood. Back over the stony road he urged his horse lest he be too late. Tethering him carefully, he crept stealthily through the trees. There were the two again. Gawaine's arms were about her, and the moonlight was upon her fair face upturned to him. They stood motionless. Pelleas gathered himself for a spring and once more drew his sword. And then something unseen held him back and, sadly, he sheathed his blade again. Once more the horse was turned campward, but this time with a more restless rider. Often he looked back and, ere he had gone far, murmured, "It must be," and wheeled again toward the castle. There were the lovers just as he had left them. Gawaine's head slowly bent over the lovely face. Their lips met. So engrossed were they that they neither saw nor heard the mail-clad figure with the naked sword that emerged from the woods. Nor did they see Pelleas bend and silently lay his sword at their feet and plunge madly into the forest. Not until he had ridden recklessly far toward his camp did Ettarre, casting down her eyes, see the gleam of the blade in the moonlight. Slowly, as if fascinated by the glittering steel, she bent and picked it up. Si-

lently she examined the hilt. Quietly, with her
eyes fixed upon Gawaine, she slipped away from
him like a wild beast that gathers herself for a
spring; quietly, but trembling in every nerve.
Gawaine watched her in amazement. Never was
a woman transformed so suddenly. She seemed
a veritable tigress in her stealthy, hardly per-
ceptible, yet rapid movement. Then she spoke,
slowly at first, and with unspeakable disdain,
then gradually more and more rapidly, until the
words became a serpent's hiss, yet always in a
half whisper: "Gawaine, false knight, this
sword is Pelleas's. He is not dead. You lied to
me, and deceived me as only a coward knows how
to lie and to deceive. Had Pelleas been you and
you he just now, you would have killed him, de-
fenseless as he was. I hated Pelleas, but he is
a man and a true knight. Go, and never let me
see you more!"

Pelleas, when he had left Ettarre and
Gawaine, set out at once for his own camp. His
heart was heavy indeed, and tears blinded his
eyes, but he rode recklessly, for his mind was
made up. Crashing through the dark underbrush, slipping over the stony beds of streams,
splashing over marsh, and floundering through
morass, his good steed speedily brought him to
his tent. His squires leaped up from the ground
where they lay about the campfire in the peaceful moonlight, startled by the sudden and dis-
ordered appearance of their master. Pelleas
hastily dismounted and, without a word, entered

his tent. Flinging off his armor, he threw himself upon his bed and called his squires. "Never shall I rise from this bed," said he wearily. "Divide among you my arms and horses, and all other things I have, and when I am gone, bury my body by the lake side. My lady and my friend have both deserted me, and there is nothing left to live for." He motioned the sorrowing squires away and, turning his face from them, gave way to his grief and wept as if his heart would break.

The night wore on. The bright moon sank behind the black trees. A light mist arose from the water and the first blush of dawn appeared on the hilltops beyond the lake. Brighter and brighter grew the sky and its glow was reflected in the calm water. The birds began to twitter a sleepy welcome to the dawn. More and more ruddy became the sky; a light breeze sprang up, cooling the faces of the tired and heartsick watchers and bringing them refreshment even in their grief. Then the sun appeared, and the birds broke into a joyous chorus. The waves lapped softly upon the pebbly beach. All the world seemed happy and at peace. But within his tent, Pelleas tossed restlessly upon his couch. His cheeks were flushed, his eyes gleamed with a wild light, and as he rolled his fevered head upon his pillow he muttered softly, "Faithless! faithless! faithless!"

The squires peeped in at the door and sorrowfully turned away. What comfort could they

give their distracted lord? Silently and aim-
lessly they loitered toward the shore, and each
wandered away along the water's edge alone.
Their grief was too deep even for companionship. And as the squire whom Sir Pelleas most
loved, walked along the shore, weeping and
moaning, a strange and unexpected thing happened. Looking up, he saw at a distance a lady
in shining white garments approaching him. So
suddenly did she appear that it seemed as if she
must have come from the water, but her clothes
were not wet, and her long, yellow hair floated
lightly in the morning breeze. As the sun shone
through it, she seemed to be surrounded by a
glory such as surrounds the saints in church
windows, and the young knight thought he had
never seen a woman so beautiful. Indeed, her
beauty seemed unearthly and more than mortal
could possess. Nearer and nearer came the
beautiful lady, and when she saw him weeping
she asked, "Why do you weep, Sir Knight, when
all this glorious world shines with peace and
happiness?"

"Alas," replied the squire, "my master has
been betrayed by the Lady Ettarre and his
friend Gawaine, and he now lies upon his bed
from which he vows never to rise. Indeed, it
were a great pity that so good and gentle a
knight as Sir Pelleas should die, but in nowise
can we persuade him to rise."

"Bring me to him," said the lady, "for I am
Nimue, a damsel of the lake, and I warrant that

your master shall not die. As for the lady, she shall soon be in as evil a plight as Pelleas is now, for it can bring no joy to such a proud lady to have no mercy on such a valiant knight."

So the squire brought Nimue to Pelleas and he related to her all his woe. Now even as he retold his tale, Pelleas moaned less and less often, for Nimue was exceedingly beautiful and gentle. She listened to his story with a sympathy that soothed his troubled heart. Far, far different was this fair lady's kindness from the studied cruelty of Ettarre. And Nimue, for her part, thought she had never seen so handsome a knight.

To Pelleas Nimue repeated her promise to win for him the affection of Ettarre. She threw him into a deep sleep by her enchantments, and left him to dream—perhaps of the proud Ettarre; perhaps of the lovely Nimue.

Quickly Nimue came to Lady Ettarre. Roundly did she reproach her for the murder of so brave and courteous a knight as Pelleas, and she cast a spell over her so that she loved Pelleas even more than he had loved her. Then Nimue and Ettarre rode straightway to Pelleas. When they arrived he was still asleep. Both ladies entered his tent, and when Ettarre saw him, so handsome yet so worn with sorrow and anguish, she was beside herself with grief and self-reproach. But when Sir Pelleas awoke and saw them standing beside him, he hated Ettarre as much as he had loved her before.

Ettarre was beside herself with grief and self-reproach.

"Away, traitress!" he cried, "come nevermore unto my sight." Despite her protestations of love and pleading for forgiveness, his heart relented not one whit. So she went away sorrowing, and some say died of grief.

"Sir Pelleas," said the damsel, "Take your horse and come with me out of this country, and you will find a lady that will truly love you."

"Gladly will I do so," replied Pelleas, "for I have suffered much here and at the hands of this false lady, Ettarre. I thank heaven I am rid of her."

"Thank me," said Nimue.

So Pelleas put on his armor and together he and Nimue rode forth into the forest, never to be separated as long as life lasted.

The Maid
of Astolat

"Then to her tower she climb'd, and took the shield,
There kept it, and so lived in fantasy."

Now it chanced that as Lady Day approached, King Arthur resolved to call a great tournament at Camelot. He announced that he and the King of the Scots would meet all comers in a great mock battle. Hastily the best and most valiant knights in all Britain, and even from beyond the sea, began to gather. Some took the side against Arthur, with the King of Northumberland and he who was known as the King with a Hundred Knights as their leaders, while in Arthur's party were King Anguish of Ireland and many of the best knights of the Round Table. Lancelot withheld his promise to take part, pleading in excuse that he had not yet recovered from a wound.

In due time the king and his friends set out for Camelot, and presently Lancelot followed, unknown to Arthur.

In the upper reaches of the Thames, and at
no great distance from the river was the little
town of Astolat, and above the town rose the
towers of the castle of old Baron Bernard. There
dwelt the worthy old knight with his two sons,
Sir Tirre and Sir Lavaine, both but lately made
knights, and his fair daughter, Elaine.

It was in the early evening when the king,
riding toward Camelot, came upon the gray towers of Bernard's castle, ruddy with the last rays
of the setting sun, rising above the little town
that nestled about the base of the hill. The fast
approaching darkness and the dusk of the tree-
sheltered valley road warned the king that he
must seek shelter for the night, so his party
spurred their way up the steep approach to the
castle, where they were met with a hearty
welcome by the hospitable old knight and his
household.

Not long after Arthur's arrival another
guest rode up to the great gate. He was alone,
but all were welcome at Astolat, and he, too, was
received most courteously. As he rode through
the courtyard, Arthur spied him and recognized
Sir Lancelot.

"I have just seen a knight who will meet us
in the coming tournament," said the king to his
knights, "and I warrant he will do marvels."

"Who is it?" asked his followers.

"I shall not tell you yet," replied Arthur, with
a smile, as he went to his chamber, but he se-
cretly resolved that Gawaine should not enter

the lists, for whenever he and Lancelot met, Gawaine was worsted.

Meanwhile the kind old Baron led Lancelot to the great hall and gave him courteous welcome. But he knew not that his guest was the great Lancelot.

"Fair sir," said Lancelot, "I would pray you lend me a shield that is not well known for the coming jousts, for mine is well known and I would joust disguised."

"That I will do gladly," said his host. "My elder son was hurt the day he was made knight, so badly, indeed, that he cannot ride. His shield is unknown anywhere but here, and you shall have that. And I, too, would pray a favor of you. My younger son here, Sir Lavaine, is a likely and strong youth, eager for adventure. I would gladly have him ride to the jousts with so noble a knight as you appear to be—I do not yet know your name."

"Right gladly would I have your son go with me," responded Lancelot heartily, "but I must ask you to forgive me if I do not tell you my name at this time. If all goes well at the tournament, I shall come back to you and then you shall know who I am. Think me not discourteous, gentle knight, for there are reasons why I must remain unknown."

Then Sir Bernard turned to his daughter, who all this time had been standing near, her eyes fixed in admiration on the handsome strange knight.

"Go, daughter, and bring your brother's shield," said he.

Presently she returned with the shield, and Lancelot handed his own to her. "Keep this shield until I come again," he said kindly. She took it like a precious thing, and little did the valiant knight dream how all the long hours he was away she would treasure it in her chamber, and muse over it, and dream upon it, yes, and press it close in her arms and kiss it, because it was his.

As she took the shield from him, she shyly asked if he would wear at the jousts a token of hers.

"Fair damsel," said Lancelot, "if I do that for you, you may truly say that I do more for you than ever I have done for any lady, for never have I worn a token from any lady before this. But I will wear your token in my helmet right gladly." He thought to himself that thus he would, indeed, be well disguised at the tournament, for all the world knew that Lancelot had never worn a lady's favor. Then Elaine brought him a crimson scarf, richly sewn with pearls. And not for an instant during the evening did her eyes leave the face of this brave and handsome knight who would wear her token in the tournament.

The next morning Arthur and his knights departed from Astolat, and soon afterward Lancelot and Sir Lavaine followed them. When they arrived at Camelot they went to the home

of a rich citizen who was a friend of Sir
Lavaine's father and there were lodged awaiting the tournament. Meantime the city was
filling with those who were to take part in and
those who were to watch the tournament. Every
house was filled; rich tents and pavilions were
pitched in the surrounding meadows; everywhere swirled the motley crowd. From the upper windows, the milling, colorful streets looked
like huge rainbows or mighty kaleidoscopes,
ever changing yet constantly bright.

But when the great tournament began, these
streets were deserted, and the whole gay throng
was packed about the lists. A truly noble array
of knights was lined up at each end of the lists
awaiting the signal from the heralds' trumpets.
The King of the Scots, King Anguish of Ireland,
the mighty Sir Palomides, Mordred, Kay, and
Griflet, to mention but a few of the most famous,
were on Arthur's side, while the King of North-
galis, the King with a Hundred Knights, the
King of Northumberland, and Sir Galahad were
against the king. Apart, on the edge of the
field, two silent figures sat their horses. Their
shields were blank; no one might guess their
names. One wore in his helmet a crimson scarf.

Again and again Arthur's knights charged.
Again and again his adversaries counter-
charged. Lance shivered upon shield, and shield
clattered to earth. Down went horses and men.
Swords were drawn, and the din of steel on steel
filled the air. Now one side, now the other

was beaten back, only to rally and come on again with renewed vigor. Broken armor, shattered spears, shorn plumes littered the ground. The ranks of both sides thinned and many a riderless horse galloped frantically among the fighters, adding to the confusion and uproar. But, by and by, Arthur's knights began to beat back their opponents with the steady persistence that to the trained eye of a soldier told the ultimate defeat of Arthur's adversaries. When he saw this, the knight of the red scarf said to his companion, "It is our time. If you will help me a little you will see the pursuers chased back as rapidly as they now come forward."

"Sir," said his comrade, "spare not. I will do what I may."

And with that, Sir Lancelot and Sir Lavaine rode into the thickest of the fight with such a mighty charge that Lancelot unhorsed four of Arthur's men before he broke his spear, and Sir Lavaine smote down two. Seizing another lance Lancelot unseated five men, and Lavaine hurled from their saddles another two. Then Lancelot drew his sword and laid about him so vigorously that many other knights were soon on the ground, and Arthur's party withdrew to the end of the lists in confusion.

"Indeed this is a most marvelous knight," said Sir Gawaine to Arthur, "and were it not for the scarf he wears in his helmet I should think it was Lancelot, for no other knight did I ever see do such deeds at arms."

"I know who he is," said the king, "we shall know him better before he leaves."

By this time the king's forces had rallied and, heartily ashamed of their late reverse, they threw themselves upon their adversaries with renewed vigor. And especially they set upon the unknown knights. Then three set at once upon Lancelot, and Lancelot's horse was killed. A spear pierced Lancelot's shield and entered his side, the point breaking off in the wound. Lavaine, reckless with rage, threw himself upon the King of Scots and, knocking him from horse, brought the charger to Lancelot and, despite the assault of all Arthur's knights, helped his fallen chief to mount. A-horse again, Lancelot, though sorely wounded, indeed fearing that he had met his death, laid about him with mighty blows and smote down many a noble knight, so that ere the joust was ended he had overcome more than thirty knights, and Sir Lavaine, on his part, did marvelously well, for he that day unhorsed ten knights, and most of these were of the Round Table.

Then the king caused the heralds to blow "to lodgings," and, after the trumpets had sounded and the knights laid down their arms, the heralds came forward with the prize to bestow it upon "the knight of the white shield and the red scarf," for as yet Lancelot was unknown to them.

Then said Lancelot: "My Lords, if I deserve thanks I have bought it at a great price, for I

am likely to lose my life through this adventure.
I am sorely hurt and beg your leave to depart,
for I had now rather have rest than be lord of
all the world."

With that, he wheeled his horse about and,
followed by Sir Lavaine, rode hastily away from
the lists. At last they came to a little wood and
there halted. Turning to Lavaine, Lancelot said
weakly, "I pray you to pull this spear from my
side, for it galls me past all endurance."

This Lavaine was loath to do, fearing that
Lancelot would bleed to death, but as Lancelot
urged, he at last seized the shattered lance, and,
with a great tug, drew it from Lancelot's side.
The wounded knight fainted. He remained in
the swoon so long that Sir Lavaine feared that
he was dead, but at last his eyes opened, and he
begged his young friend to take him to a certain
hermit not far away who was a skilful physician.

Presently they arrived at the hermitage
which was a large and comfortable house set in
a pleasant wood, for the hermit was a rich
knight who had renounced the world through
piety. There they were courteously received and,
though the patient was unknown, the hermit
undertook to treat his wound. But when the
wounded knight removed his helmet, his physician recognized him as Lancelot, and doubled
his efforts to make him comfortable and to re-
pair his hurt.

While Lancelot lay at the hermit's forest retreat, Arthur and his knights were seeking him.

All agreed that so great a knight should not
have been permitted to go away in such a des-
perate plight as he had left the lists, and not a
few hinted that he had been foully dealt with.
All admired him, though none but Arthur knew
his name, and even those who had fared worst
at his hands in the tournament had nothing but
praise for the brave and able knight. "By my
head," exclaimed Sir Gawaine, "I will find him."
Forthwith, he set out, accompanied by a squire,
to scour the country. Into all the highways and
byways about Camelot he went, and sought out
all the retreats where a wounded man would be
likely to go. Nowhere, however, could he find
a trace of the knight of the red scarf. Then
Arthur set out for London, and Sir Gawaine set
out on a longer search more distant from Camelot. And so one evening he came to the castle
of Sir Bernard and sought shelter for the night.
Of course, it was readily given him, and news of
the court and especially of the tournament was
eagerly inquired for by his host. You may be
sure that Lady Elaine had plenty of questions to
ask about the jousts.

"There were two knights," answered Sir
Gawaine, "who bore white shields, and one of
them wore a red scarf upon his helmet, and certainly he was one of the best knights that ever I
saw joust, for I dare say he smote down forty
knights of the Round Table. His companion did
right well, too, and perhaps saved his comrade's
life."

Then Elaine in her innocence frankly told Gawaine the story of the knight of the red scarf and how he had left his shield in her keeping but had refused to tell them his name.

"Show me the shield," said Gawaine.

So the shield was brought and the case which covered it was pulled off.

"Lancelot!" exclaimed Gawaine. And, in his turn, he told how Lancelot had been wounded and how he and his companion had ridden away, nobody knew where. And Elaine was very proud to know that her token had been worn by the knight of greatest prowess in the tournament, and that Sir Lancelot, who had never before worn a lady's token, had worn hers. Nevertheless, her tender heart was filled with sadness by the news of his hurt and she pictured him to herself wandering wounded, perhaps dying, with only her brother for a companion, nobody knew where.

"Father," she cried, "let me seek Sir Lancelot and my brother, for never can I be happy until I find them." Then her father fitted her out for traveling, and she set off and by chance found her brother at Camelot, where he had gone to have his horse shod, and with him rode to the hermitage where Lancelot lay. Sir Lavaine led her to Lancelot's chamber, and when she saw him lying there so weak and pale, who late had been so strong and full of life, she fainted. The brave knight was deeply touched by her devotion. Calling her to him he kissed her, and as she sat beside him learned how she had found out who he was and how she had sought him out. And the days passed happily for the wounded man and for his devoted nurse. Elaine never left his side and was ever eager to do what she might for his comfort. At last Lancelot was fully recovered of his wound and joyfully he rode beside Elaine and Lavaine to their father's house. Sir Bernard received them with great rejoicing, and there Lancelot remained a little while before returning to Arthur's court. But when he was about to leave, the lovely Elaine came to him and begged him to take her with him.

"Take me with you," she begged, "even as a servant, for I cannot live when you are away from me."

"That I cannot, fair maid," said Lancelot sadly, for his heart was deeply touched by her devotion.

"Truly I shall die, if you leave me," pleaded Elaine, and despite Lancelot's attempts to comfort her she burst into tears and, weeping softly, climbed the stairs to her chamber. From its window she watched the departing knight in whom her whole soul was wrapped up. Slowly his horse bore him along the road which they had so joyfully ridden together a few days before. Smaller and smaller became his figure in the distance. At last it crossed a little hill and was gone. But the maid of Astolat gazed long from her window. The stars came out and faded,

and still she remained looking toward Camelot
and dreaming of Lancelot. And when the morning came, she lay down on her bed and called for
her father and her elder brother.

"My heart is breaking," said she, "and I soon
shall die. Let Sir Tirre write as I shall dictate
and let the writing be placed in my hand after I
am dead. Then place my body on a barge draped
in black, and put at the helm a trusted servant,
and let the barge drift down the Thames to
Westminster."

Then she directed what her brother should
write, and presently she died.

Astolat and all the country roundabout was
filled with sorrow by the death of this gentle
lady, for her goodness was of equal fame with
her beauty. Castle and peasant's hut were alike
filled with grief, and willing hands hastened to
prepare the funeral barge as Elaine had re-
quested. They draped it with black satin and
with the flowers that Elaine had loved, and when
it was done they placed the body of the unhappy
lady, clad in her richest robes, upon a rich bed
covered with cloth of gold in the midst of the
barge. An old retainer of the family, clad in
black, took the long steering oar, and the peas-
ants pushed the boat into the current of the
Thames. Slowly it drifted down the stream,
while the weeping friends of poor Elaine stood
upon the bank and watched the receding barge
until it had become a black speck on the shining
river.

Gaily passed the days at Westminster where
Arthur held his court. All the Knights of the
Round Table had gathered, and tales of adventures that they had experienced in their jour-
neys entertained and thrilled the court. The
great Lancelot, still shaken and weak from his
wounds, the healing of which he had delayed by
rash practice at arms before his side was fully
knit, was there. His valorous conduct when, as
a disguised knight, he had entered the great
tournament was on every tongue. But his soul
was heavy for he thought often of the Fair Maid
of Astolat, and his brave and gentle heart was
grieved because through him she had been
brought so great sorrow. He pictured her
mourning in her lonely chamber high over
sleepy little Astolat, nursing a hopeless love.
Truly would he be glad to hear that she had
found a new love, and he promised himself that
if she did, he would dower her handsomely. But
he was alone in his grief and about him all was
merriment and the court echoed with light
laughter.

Now one day as they were strolling by the
Thames, two knights espied a black dot, far up
the river. Lazily it drifted toward them, well
out in the middle of the stream, but, as it approached Westminster and began to draw near
the bank, the watchers saw that it was a barge,
heavily draped with black satin which trailed
behind it in the water. In the stern stood an old
man, bent over the long steering sweep. Won-

dering what the strange boat might mean, the knights followed it until it touched the river bank. No one alighted from it; no word could they get from the aged man at the oar. Cautiously they peeped through the curtains. There, upon a rich bed, they beheld the loveliest lady they had ever seen, clothed in rich robes and strewn with garlands. They turned away, awestruck, and hastened to the king.

Quickly the gaiety of the court was turned to curiosity and the curiosity to grief as the knights related their story, and Arthur and his queen and all his courtiers hastened to the river side. Arthur and Guineviere alone entered the barge and found all as the knights had described it. Great was their sorrow, and gladly would they have learned who the fair girl was and why she had been brought thus to Westminster, but the lone old helmsman only bowed speechless in grief over the handle of his oar.

And then the queen espied a paper clasped in Elaine's hand. Arthur took it and the whole train returned again to the court. There, before all the courtiers, Arthur broke the seal. Lancelot had come in, having heard of the king's errand, with Sir Lavaine and others who had not been to the black barge. Slowly the king read, and as he read all eyes were turned on Lancelot, for the paper told of poor Elaine's unreturned love for the great knight and the heartbreak that had brought her death. And the greathearted Lancelot buried his face in his hands, and wept that such a fate should have befallen so fair a lady through him. Her brother, before the whole court, absolved Lancelot of any blame for her death, but this was small balm to the troubled heart of the generous knight. But in recompense for her devotion—a poor thing, but all that he could do—he caused her to be richly buried at Westminster, and all the knights and ladies of the court attended poor Elaine's funeral mass.

Then the black barge turned up the Thames and the solitary boatman slowly rowed it back toward Astolat. Slowly, slowly the black boat glided up the stream, until it was a black speck on the shining water. So ends the tale of the Maid of Astolat.

The Passing of
King Arthur

"Hail, King! tomorrow thou shalt pass away.
Farewell! there is an isle of rest for thee."

GREAT changes had taken place at King
Arthur's court since the coming of Sir
Galahad. The knights were all vowed, now, to
search for the Holy Grail that had disappeared
from the castle of King Pelles when Sir Galahad
went away. Who had taken it? everybody
asked; but no one could give a reply. Had it
really been carried through the banqueting hall
the night that Sir Galahad had taken his place
upon the Seat Perilous? Or was it only a dream,
a vision, that the knights had seen? If it were
a vision, would any of them see it again? They
could not answer these questions; but, one and
all, they sought for the Shining Cup during the
rest of their lives.

Joseph and the Rich Fisher had long ago
passed away, you see, and perhaps they alone
knew what the Holy Grail really was. The

strange old minstrel with the two bright snakes
around his neck knew just a little but not everything. He wore the snakes to show that he
belonged to the old, old order of bards—the men
who were something like priests and who sang
stories of great nations and greater kings. His
Song of the Holy Grail was written down in the
little book that he must have found in Merlin's
mysterious house with the seventy windows and
the sixty doors. For Merlin was one of these
bards himself and very likely wore bright
snakes about his neck as he came and went at
King Arthur's court, though we are not exactly
told that he ever did. But then we are by no
means told all that happened in those days, and
if we were, perhaps we should not believe it.
This we do know, however, that all the knights
who searched for the lost Grail Cup knew that
they had no chance of finding it, or even catching a glimpse of it in a vision, unless they were
thoroughly good and true and pure, and without
reproach. So all of them tried hard to be so;
and, though none of them ever quite succeeded,
the very trying made their lives beautiful—just
as shining and beautiful as the silver armor they
wore and the spears and swords that they carried in their hands.

They still met at the Round Table, still
passed the Cup of Fellowship from hand to hand,
but the king, as he sat among them, felt that he
was growing old. His eyes were often heavy,
and his feet and hands grew tired when he

donned his shining armor and wielded his famous sword. And one day he was obliged to go into battle against an enemy when he was too weary to fight. He was struck down and wounded, and his faithful knights carried him to a quiet, grassy place in a meadow near which rippled the shining waters of a great lake.

King Arthur lay on the moss with his fingers on the handle of his sword Excalibur, and his followers stood around him with sad faces, for they thought that death was about to take their beloved king. But he himself knew better. He smiled as he lay there, and his face was very bright. Lifting himself up a little he looked toward the waters of the lake, and then he beckoned to a knight who was called Sir Bedivere.

"Take my sword Excalibur," said he. "Throw it as far as you can fling it toward the center of the lake. Then come back and tell me what happens."

Sir Bedivere took the sword and carried it to the edge of the lake. Night was falling, and the moon was brightening above the quiet hills. In the moonlight the jewels in the handle of Excalibur looked very rich and beautiful—so rich and so beautiful that Sir Bedivere felt he could not bear to throw the sword into the water. He hid it among the forget-me-nots and meadowsweet, and went, empty-handed, back to the king.

"Did you throw the sword into the lake?" asked Arthur eagerly.

"Yes, sire," answered Sir Bedivere boldly.
"What happened?"

"Nothing happened, sire!"

The king lay back again with a groan.

"Faithless messenger!" he said. "You have not thrown the sword! Go! Do as I command you."

Again Sir Bedivere went, but again the beauty of Excalibur overcame him. He returned to the king, and declared that he had flung the sword into the water, but still nothing had happened.

Arthur looked at him steadily, and his eyes made Sir Bedivere tremble.

"You are not speaking the truth!" cried the king. "Go! Do as I command!"

His voice was very strong and stern, and at last Bedivere obeyed. Hurrying to the water's edge he took Excalibur in his hand again, this time not daring to look at its beauty. The rubies and sapphires and diamonds of the handle flashed as he flung it far, far into the lake. Just as it was about to strike the water a white hand and arm, clothed in a shining sleeve, rose above the ripples, and the outstretched fingers caught the sword. Three times the hand waved Excalibur in the moonlight—then arm and sword disappeared below the water, and all was still.

Breathless and awed, Sir Bedivere went back to the king and told what he had seen.

"It is well!" said Arthur wearily. "Carry me to the lake!"

The outstretched fingers caught the sword.

So his knights lifted him and carried him gently across the moonlit grass, until they came to the water's edge. As they walked in slow procession they saw a dim ship, like a dark barge, coming from the middle of the lake toward the bank. Many ladies, shadowy in the pale light, were seated in it, with their heads bowed upon their hands. All of them were hooded; and three, who wore crowns upon their heads, looked like queens.

Then the king bade the knights lay him in the barge, and they did so, and gave him into the care of the three queens.

"So to the barge they came. There those three queens
Put forth their hands, and took the King, and wept."

Down from the hills swept a great wind— and it seemed as if the sound of sobbing and wailing was in its cold breath. The clouds rushed across the moon, and the water of the lake looked black and terrible as the barge began to move away from the land. The knights stood upon the bank and watched as if they were in a dream.

Then, even as they watched, the darkness went away. Far, far off, right away, as it were, beyond the mere, little shining islands began to show, bright and beautiful and for all the world like sunset clouds. All the knights had heard of these islands, and knew that they were called the Isles of the Blest. In the very center of them

was one named Avalon, the fairest of them all.
Its valleys were fragrant with flowers, and in its
orchard grew trees that bore golden apples. It
seemed to the knights that the barge with the
three fairy queens and the weary human king
sailed right up to the shores of Avalon, and that
a number of bright and beautiful people came
to meet it.

> "Then from the dawn it seem'd there came, but faint
> As from beyond the limit of the world,
> Like the last echo bore of a great cry,
> Sounds, as if some fair city were one voice
> Around a king returning from his wars."

Then the whole vision faded. Nothing was
left but the lake and the moonlit meadows and
the memory of the great and only King of the
Round Table.

But some people say that Arthur lives and is
happy in Avalon to this day, and that there he
has met Joseph, and the Rich Fisher, and his old
wise teacher, Merlin, the great magician. They
say, too, that it is in Avalon that the Silver Table
is hidden, on which stands the Shining Cup; and
that there, every evening is held the mysterious
feast which fills all the guests with joy and
amazement, just as they were filled with joy and
amazement hundreds of years ago on that
Christmas Day when Joseph's staff broke into
blossom at Glastonbury.